P9-DED-841

NOWHERE

TO RUN

ALSO BY MARY JANE CLARK

Do You Want to Know a Secret?

Do You Promise Not to Tell?

Let Me Whisper in Your Ear

Close to You

Nobody Knows

NOWHERE TO RUN

MARY JANE CLARK

ST. MARTIN'S PRESS NEW YORK

This is a work of fiction. All the characters and events portrayed in this book are either products of the author's imagination or are used fictitiously.

ISBN 0-312-28877-8

Printed in the USA

And again, for Elizabeth and David
and
for the achievable dream of finding a treatment or cure
for the most common inherited form of mental impairment,
Fragile X syndrome.

ACKNOWLEDGMENTS

It was her idea and I thought it was an exciting one. When Laura Dail, my agent, suggested that I write something that featured a lockdown at KEY News, a situation where neither victim nor killer could escape, I pounced on the idea. Laura's fertile idea was full of possibilities for suspense.

By the time the ten-page synopsis was delivered to my editor, Jennifer Enderlin, a little anthrax had been sprinkled into the story mix. Jen gave her palpable enthusiasm to the proposal along with excellent suggestions about the potential characters and the things that might happen to them along the way. Once Jen gave the green light, there was really nowhere to run. I had to write the book.

Enter Elizabeth Kaledin. How many people are lucky enough to have a friend who sticks with them through thick and thin and who also has a reporter's notebook full of information on a weapon of mass destruction? Elizabeth does, as medical correspondent for *The CBS Evening News* with Dan Rather, and she willingly shared both her research and recollections with me. When I worried that I may have bitten off more than I could chew, Elizabeth reassured me and supported me, as she has so many times over the years.

Time frames, symptoms, and treatments for anthrax exposure had to be accurate. Dr. Angelo Acquista, Medical Director of the New York City Office of Emergency Management and author of *The Survival Guide: What to Do in a Biological, Chemical, or Nuclear Emergency*, helped me as well, gracious and generous with his time and expertise.

As he has done before, Stan Romaine, Director of CBS Corporate Security, came to my rescue. Stan listened to my fictional scenario and, over lunch and perhaps more phone conversations than he had counted on, offered myriad possibilities for tension and intrigue in my besieged TV news world. Thank you so much, Stan. You were very patient with me and your input added so much to the story.

I am constantly amazed at and grateful for the people who step up to the plate when asked. CBS News friends freely contributed. Terri Belli, B.J. D'Elia (another B.J., not the one in the book), Jerry Mazza, and Jim Murphy each supplied facts and color I hungered for and devoured.

Roberta Golubock, childhood friend and real estate maven, dropped everything at my call one Sunday morning and took me on a tour of Greenwich Village, pointing out some of the places that ended up in this book. Doing research with Roberta makes work fun. This wasn't the first time Roberta has been there to guide me, and I am confident and glad it won't be the last.

Walter Timpone, former Assistant U.S. Attorney, filled me in on the legal ramifications for the actions of one of my misguided characters. Walter immediately grasped the situation, quickly assessing the consequences and explaining them well to this unlawful mind.

At St. Martin's Press, along with my dynamo editor, Jen Enderlin, there is a wonderful team willing and eager to help. Allow me to thank Sally Richardson, Matthew Shear, Ed Gabrielli, John Karle, and John Murphy for all they have done and continue to do. A special thanks to Anne Twomey for keeping at it until this cover was just right.

Colleen Kenny, *gracias, amiga,* for your creation of and conscientious work on our website: *www.maryjaneclark.com.* You continue to surprise and delight me, Col.

Father Paul Holmes, what can I say? You have a mind that does not quit and I am the beneficiary of it. You are a stickler for detail and help make sure that I leave no thread dangling. Until the very end, your tireless support is crucial. Thank you, thank you, Paul.

And now, the work is done. To the family and friends I have neglected, I am free to run now, anywhere we choose.

NOWHERE

TO RUN

PROLOGUE

Friday, November 14

The silver New Jersey Transit commuter train slid to a stop at the red brick station. Only one passenger alighted. Pulling the overcoat collar up against the brisk night wind, the passenger stood on the platform, trying to get some bearings. The passenger pulled a folded piece of paper from a coat pocket and opened the computer-printed directions.

On the walk to the stairwell, images of the friendly cohosts of *KEY to America* smiled from a billboard illuminated by the station lights. There was no escaping those two. Constance Young and Harry Granger. They were everywhere.

Down the concrete stairs and through the spray-painted tunnel beneath the railroad tracks, past the graffitied messages. A hand-drawn eyeball wept from the cement wall with tears marked FEAR, ANGER, ANGUISH, and TERROR, as if the artist had somehow known that those emotions were the very ones to bring the traveler to this comfortable town tonight.

Another set of stairs led up to the main street. Friday night moviegoers were filing out of the old Maplewood Theatre. It was easy to mingle among them, eavesdropping on their critiques of the film that was setting box-office records.

The post office sat across the street. It would have been so easy to go that route instead of hand-delivering the envelope that lay triple-wrapped in plastic inside the coat pocket. But those poor postal workers had already been through enough. The goal tonight was not to reach some random target. This time, the lethal white powder was intended for one very specific person.

At the first corner, the smell of roasting garlic wafted from the Village Trattoria, inviting passersby to come and enjoy the delectable pleasures that waited inside. But there was no chance for that now, or even for a cup of coffee from the nearby Maple Leaf Diner. It was important to stick to the plan and return to the station in time to make the 12:39 back to Manhattan.

Plush stuffed turkeys and overflowing cornucopias decorated the windows of the gift shop on the corner of Highland Place. A baseball cap was donned as the right-hand turn was made, as the map indicated. Past the liquor store and Cent' Anni and a much-too-quick perusal of its menu. OSSO BUCO MILANESE: VEAL SHANK WITH RISOTTO AND SAFFRON. *Mmmm.* They were eating well in the 'burbs.

Out of the business district now, the road began to incline. One wooden Victorian-style house followed another, each nestled behind well-established shrubs and giant old trees. Porch lights revealed the odd numbers on the right-hand side of the street. A teenager walking a dog passed. A double sneeze in the cold night air.

Straining legs reached the very top of the hill. Number 31 was the last house. The streetlamp cast enough light to see the house number, but there was no light coming from within the house.

He wasn't home. *Perfect.*

It couldn't be going better. After a furtive look around the deserted street, it took just a few seconds to unwrap the stamped envelope and stash it in the mailbox on the porch landing.

Back at the station, with time to spare, the leather gloves were peeled off, along with the nitrile ones beneath them. Both sets were plunked in the deep trash barrel that rested on the platform, just as the city-bound train rumbled into view.

Saturday, November 15

The phone rang all morning. Well-wishers celebrating his thirty-sixth birthday. But there was no call from Annabelle.

He pulled on his sweatpants and tied his running shoes, determined to get some exercise, get those endorphins pulsing and work off that beer he'd guzzled the night before. He was feeling strong and optimistic that in the year to come things were really going to start going his way again. With his manuscript finished and the prospects for selling it good, his spirits were high. He well knew what made a best-seller, and his project had all the earmarks of a hit.

The fun part was imagining what he was going to do with all that money. Maybe, on his thirty-seventh birthday, he'd fly some friends down to the islands to bask and party in the Caribbean sun. If only Annabelle could come along.

At first, the cold air shocked him; then he welcomed it as his body temperature rose. The last of the leaves floated from the elms and pin oaks, landing on the pavement beneath his feet. He panted as he hit his stride, soft clouds of white, steamy breath puffing from his nostrils. It was good to be alive.

After completing his three-mile circuit, he stopped for a cup of coffee and bought a newspaper, walking the rest of the way home, cooling down. By habit, he checked his mailbox, finding only a lone envelope inside. He had expected more on his birthday.

He went into the house, kicked off his running shoes, and collapsed in his favorite upholstered armchair. Examining the purple envelope, addressed in an unfamiliar hand, he speculated that the sender might be a female and, for an instant, he fantasized that Annabelle had sent it.

His eyes wandered to the silver-framed picture that he still kept on the mantel. He had taken it at the water's edge in Bay Head. Annabelle, caught grinning as a wave knocked against her, the sun shining on her brunette head, her white teeth flashing and her blue eyes sparkling against her sun-tanned face. She'd complained about her freckles and wished for thinner thighs. He'd laughed and teased her. Didn't she know by now? He liked his women with some meat on their bones.

The two birthdays he had spent with her had been his happiest by far. But those were years ago. Now, Annabelle had married someone else and mothered two little kids while he lived as a bachelor in this house he had inherited from his parents. He supposed it was an okay life, as lives went. He had an interesting job and was paid well to do it. He had a book that could take off big time, friends to share happy times with, and good health to enjoy it all with. But as the years went by, he doubted more and more that he'd ever find the right mate. None of the women he dated ever seemed able to meet his exacting requirements—the "Annabelle" standard.

Intrigued, he held the letter to his nose. Musky, almost intoxicating. There was no return address. A stamp was affixed but not postmarked. Maybe the post office had fouled up and hadn't inked it. Or maybe someone had meant to mail it but decided to drop it off instead. He hoped it was the latter. That would mean the mailman hadn't delivered the rest of the mail yet.

He ripped open the flap and pulled out the card. A

shower of shiny silver confetti spilled from inside, falling onto his sweatpants and shirt. He brushed the tiny bits of paper away, glad that the cleaning woman had asked if she could come in on Saturday this week.

It was signed, A SECRET ADMIRER.

He took another long whiff, trying to conjure up an image of the dream woman who might smell this way. *No.* He shook himself. He had promised himself to swear off females for a while. They were too much work, and he couldn't be distracted.

With resolve, he tossed the card into the trash basket, but not before taking one last, long sniff.

THURSDAY

NOVEMBER 20

CHAPTER

1

As Mike slid back into their bed, Annabelle got out of it, not bothering to ask him where he'd been or what he'd been doing. Another sleepless night for him, another lonely one for her. It was the rhythm of their lives now.

Closing the bedroom door behind her, she switched on the lamps to brighten the early morning grayness and headed for the kitchen. Two plastic lunch boxes, one red, one blue, lay open on the counter. Annabelle placed a bologna sandwich, a bag of pretzels, and a small box of raisins inside each one and tucked a paper napkin on top. As the kettle whistle began to hiss, she whisked it from the burner, lest its screech wake the kids. She had fifteen minutes before she had to rouse Thomas and Tara to get ready for school. Fifteen minutes of treasured quiet that she was not eager to give up.

She wrapped her fingers around the warmth of the ceramic mug and took a sip of the steaming green tea, wincing as the scalding liquid hit her tongue. The taste did nothing for her, but she took comfort in the idea that it was good for her, that she was doing something to fortify and cleanse herself. She knew she had to take care of Annabelle. No one else was going to now. With Mike the way he was, if she got sick too, the whole house of cards would come tumbling down.

In bare feet, she padded across the living room and switched on the television set, making sure to keep the volume down. Her piece was scheduled to air during the first half hour of *KEY to America,* and she didn't want to miss it. This one had been a bear. It had entailed doing hours of research on an unfamiliar subject, obtaining the proper permissions to shoot, setting up for interviews and ordering video material, writing the script because her correspondent was too busy and preoccupied to do it himself, and working extra hours to make sure the story was edited on time. Right now, John Lee, M.D., KEY News medical correspondent, would be sitting uptown in the Broadcast Center, having his makeup applied, champing at the bit to go on national television and take all the credit for her hard work.

But that was what it was to be Lee's producer. While Annabelle thought Lee was an ambitious horse's behind, less devoted to the Hippocratic oath than to parlaying his national television visibility into book deals, product endorsements, and an even bigger TV contract the next time around, she accepted her role of making him look good. She wanted to keep this job. She needed it. Mike's disability payments from the city weren't enough to keep their family going.

As the theme music of the morning news program began

to play, Annabelle marveled that she was working at KEY News again. When she left after two miscarriages, followed by fertility treatments that led to the birth of the twins, she hadn't expected to return full-time to the Broadcast Center ever again. She had worked too hard to have her babies, and she wanted to enjoy raising them. Mike's salary and overtime from the fire department, her occasional freelance producing or writing assignments, and a precious rent-stabilized apartment had allowed them to get by for the last six years.

It had been a golden time.

A strong, vital husband, with a great sense of humor and a quick wit, two healthy children, and a home full of warmth and laughter. Annabelle was glad, now, as she pulled her red flannel robe closer around her and gazed out the window, that she had appreciated those days, lived them fully, reveled in them. So oblivious were they of what was to come. Annabelle watched below as a lumbering street-cleaning truck brushed litter and dirt from the Perry Street curb, while a few early risers strode purposefully toward their destinations. A fat black pigeon landed on the railing of the iron fire escape. A morning like so many others in Greenwich Village, before and after everything happened.

A quick glance at the clock on the bookcase told her that it was time to go in and wake the kids. She turned up the volume on the television set to ensure that she would hear the lead-in to her piece and headed to the twins' bedroom.

As she beheld the two little heads that lay cradled against the Barney pillowcases, Annabelle stopped, wondering yet again if she would ever get over the magic of having these fabulous creatures in her life. Rough-and-tumble Thomas, so quick to laugh, so eager to please. Thoughtful and artistic Tara, quieter and more complicated than her brother but, as Annabelle's mother used to say, "full of the devil." Two children who were conceived in such love and hope, and whose existence had exceeded their parents' most cherished dreams.

She smiled and shook her head as she watched Thomas raise his thumb to his mouth in sleep. During the day, her son was trying so hard to break the habit, but he was addicted to the comfort of it. In the whole scheme of things, what did it really matter, she asked herself, watching his gullet move beneath the soft skin of his throat as he sucked. He would give it up when he was ready to give it up. As a matter of fact, sometimes she felt like crawling under the covers and sucking her thumb herself. But she couldn't. Thomas and Tara needed at least one parent who was acting like one.

She hated herself for the resentment she had been feeling lately. At first, she had been understanding of and sympathetic to Mike's uncharacteristic dark moods and long, chilly silences. After what he had been through, it was all too predictable that he'd shut down. He'd been there, seen it, lost close friends, and attended too many funerals to count. The ghosts of the dead hovered in the firehouse.

But his depression had been going on for too long now.

Though Mike was dutifully attending his mandatory counseling sessions, "cuckoo time" he called it, Annabelle didn't see any improvement. He didn't want to leave the apartment, didn't want to ride an elevator, shuddered when he heard an airplane fly overhead. What hurt her most was observing his lack of interest in the children and seeing the puzzled, hurt expressions on their faces when Daddy refused to give them their baths or read them a favorite bedtime story. It fell on Annabelle to plug all the parental gaps and explain to the twins that, while Daddy wasn't feeling well now, he would surely be better soon, soothing them as she tried to convince herself.

She hoped the medication would kick in soon. It had been over two weeks since Mike had started on the new prescription. There had been no change Annabelle could observe.

She bent down and touched her daughter's thin shoulder. Tara's round, blue eyes popped open. The child was disoriented for only a moment, quickly recognizing her mother's face and taking in her surroundings. She sat upright, brushing her fine, tangled brown hair back from her forehead, and reached for the cardboard shoe box she had carefully placed at the foot of the twin bed the night before.

"There it is, honey. All set for show-and-tell today."

"Good," said the child, opening the lid and inspecting the contents, as she had so many times before going to sleep last night.

"You did a beautiful job on those, Tara, you really did." Annabelle reached in to take one of the painted leaves from the box. As she examined it, she uttered a silent prayer of thanks that Mrs. Nuzzo had taken the kids to the playground yesterday afternoon, scouring it for the dried leaves and then supervising the painting activities. Every Thursday's show-and-tell got to be a real challenge for the parents, coming up with something new for the kids to bring in to share with the first-grade class. Annabelle had been relieved when she got home late from work the night before that this was one parental task she was being spared. Yet another part of her was envious of Mrs. Nuzzo. Gathering leaves with her children and sitting at the kitchen table to decorate them sounded exceedingly sweet.

"Thomas, big guy, time to get up." The boy pulled his thumb from his mouth and clamped his eyelids shut. "Come on, Thomas. If you get up right away, we'll have time to have French toast," Annabelle cajoled. "Otherwise it's Cheerios again."

"And sausage?" the child asked, keeping his eyes closed.

Annabelle fought the temptation to lie to him as an incentive to get him out of bed. "No, honey, sausage is for the weekend. But the French toast will be all nice and warm and syrupy. Just the way you like it. Come on now, get up."

The child gave in to the inevitable, swinging his pajama-clad legs over the side of his bed and pulling his knit Spider Man-emblazoned top over his head. Annabelle left the kids to dress themselves in the clothes they had laid out the night before as she heard Constance Young's voice coming from the TV in the living room.

Blond, expertly made up, and dressed in an electric blue suit, Constance was looking great again this morning. Annabelle was proud of the friend she had made in her first life at KEY News, when they'd both been starting out, Annabelle as a researcher and Constance as a young reporter. Constance had stayed the course, covering long stakeouts, volunteering for the stories none of the seasoned correspondents wanted to do, paying her dues. While Annabelle was home with her kids, Constance had devoted herself to her professional passion. Now she was cohosting the nation's highly rated morning program and making seven figures a year. Constance was beautiful, smart, successful, and unhateable because she was such a damned nice person.

If not for Constance, Annabelle doubted that she would be working at KEY News again. It was Constance who, upon hearing what was going on with Annabelle, put in the good word to the executive producer Linus Nazareth to hire her. Annabelle knew the producer had no use for mommy trackers, and she was sure Nazareth had decided to take her on just to keep his popular star happy. If Constance Young wanted Annabelle, then Annabelle was in.

Annabelle had been working her tail off to prove herself and satisfy Nazareth's latest ringing directive to "make bioterrorism sexy. Seduce me. Tell me why I should care and what I can do to save myself. Keep me and all the mommies at home riveted to our television sets lest our babies lose their lives." With those twisted marching orders, Annabelle had been forced to become all too knowledgeable about botulism, smallpox, tularemia, and plague.

As she cracked eggs over the rim of a stainless-steel mixing bowl, Annabelle listened to Constance's introduction.

"Now, in our continuing series 'What you need to know about bioterrorism,' KEY News Medical Correspondent Dr. John Lee reports this morning on anthrax. You may be surprised at what he's found."

Annabelle turned to watch as the videotape rolled and a cluster of rod-shaped bacteria lit up the television screen.

"Anthrax is the perfect killer, invisible and silent," began Dr. Lee's smooth voice. "But actually anthrax is a livestock disease and, usually, humans contract it through contact with diseased animals or their hides."

The image on the television switched to a medical textbook picture of an ugly, black scab on a human hand.

"Though anthrax spores can be ingested if infected livestock is eaten, most human infection, ninety-five percent of it, is through skin contact—what we call cutaneous anthrax. A small pimple or ulcer grows into a coal-like lesion. In fact, anthrax got its name because an infection looks like anthracite or coal. The good news is, while potentially deadly, cutaneous anthrax is highly treatable with antibiotics.

"But by far the deadliest form of anthrax is inhalation anthrax. Once someone has breathed anthrax spores into their lungs, flulike symptoms will appear. A fever, cough, body aches—symptoms that don't normally send you running to the doctor. But if there is no aggressive antibiotic treatment, the fever will elevate, breathing will become labored, and the body will go into shock."

The doctor Annabelle had interviewed the week before at New York Hospital was identified on the screen and offered his expertise: "When this severe stage sets in, it is almost always too late for a cure."

Now, Lee appeared on the screen and began walking through a laboratory. "But anthrax, as it exists in nature, is not the perfect weapon. Purifying and concentrating the anthrax spores and weaponizing them, causing those purified spores to separate so they can linger in the air and be inhaled, requires real laboratory skill. There is no way to account for all the anthrax strains that exist. Hundreds of scientists and technicians can get ahold of anthrax, and they know how to weaponize it."

The medical correspondent paused to rest his hand on a piece of machinery on the lab bench. "One of the steps in making the powdered, airy form of anthrax is freeze-drying the spores. A tabletop freeze dryer can be purchased for under eight thousand dollars. So you see, the notion that only a state-sponsored biological weapons program could produce weapons-grade anthrax is a misconception."

As the report ended, Thomas came out of the bedroom, shoes in hand. Annabelle bent down to tie his sneaker but looked up in time to catch Dr. Lee, live on the set, holding up a tiny vial of white powder.

"Constance, we'd all like to think that anthrax is so dangerous, so deadly, that it must be well guarded, impossible, we hope, for anyone with evil intentions to get his hands on. But what I have here is a test tube containing weapons-grade anthrax. I can't tell you how I got it, but if I could get it, so could other people. This is a weapon you can use and you can hide."

Annabelle watched openmouthed, not believing what she was seeing. The camera closed in on the vial, then pulled back to Constance, who shrank back in her seat across from the medical correspondent.

"What's wrong, Mommy?" asked Thomas.

"Nothing, sweetie. But Daddy is going to have to get up and walk you guys to school this morning. Mommy has to get in to work."

CHAPTER

2

The president of KEY News sat at her kitchen table, drinking her second cup of black coffee and scanning the OpEd page of *The New York Times* while keeping an ear on the television set playing in the background.

"...What I have here is a test tube containing weapons-grade anthrax. I can't tell you how I got it, but if I could get it, so could other people."

Yelena Gregory's head whipped around to view the medical correspondent proudly displaying his booty. Linus had gone too far this time. She grabbed the telephone and punched in the numbers of the Broadcast Center control room.

"Gregory for Nazareth," she barked. It took three seconds for the executive producer to get on the line.

"Linus, damn it, what's going on? Why wasn't I informed about this?" she demanded.

"Don't worry, Yelena. Don't worry. We have everything under control here."

"So that means you approved this?"

There was a momentary pause on the line as the executive producer pondered his response.

"Linus?" Her anger grew as she watched the diaper commercial that was playing on the screen. *That's nice. Real nice.* All those mothers at home, scared out of their wits that any nut could get ahold of a tube of anthrax. The diaper company sponsor should love having its commercial airing right after this piece of happy news.

"No, I didn't know Lee was going to do this, Yelena," he answered.

"Then you *don't* have everything under control, do you, Linus?"

"Yelena, I think you're overreacting."

"Oh you do, do you? That's rich. Do you have any idea the headaches this is going to cause? The police and feds are not going to be amused at our antics with a weapon of mass destruction, and our employees are going to freak out with worry that they've been exposed to spores of death. But that's nice, Linus, I'm overreacting."

Linus was calm. "I'm sure Legal can deal with the cops and the feds, and everyone at the Broadcast Center will take their cue from you, Yelena. If you reassure them that they are in no danger, that will go a long way."

"I'm glad you know what I have to do to clean up your mess, Linus. That's mighty smart of you." Yelena knocked over her coffee cup, its contents spilling across the newspaper. "Who the hell was the producer on this segment anyway?"

"Annabelle Murphy."

"Did she know about this?"

"I don't think so. At least she never told me about it."

"Well, she should have."

CHAPTER 3

Clara Romanski lay beneath her soft handmade quilt, trying to concentrate on the television as a distraction from how miserable she was feeling. The fever was getting worse. But it would pass, surely it would pass. Her immune system wasn't all it should be. She could count on getting sick several times over the winter months. Cleaning all those houses and being exposed to everybody's germs contributed to her illnesses, but she had no choice. She had to make a living somehow.

Actually, she liked all her jobs. The people she cleaned for were usually at their own jobs and their children were in school when she came to vacuum, dust, and polish their homes. She could work at her own speed, with no one watching over her shoulder. It suited her just fine.

Sometimes, though, as she iced her sore back or sat in a hot tub at night to warm the ache out of her bones, she wondered how long she could go on doing housework. After all, she was fifty-eight years old. But with no husband or children and no Social Security to look forward to, she had to depend on her savings to support her in her old age. She took any extra work she could get to add money to her retirement account.

Last week, she had overdone it. Now she was paying for it. Yes, that was it. She'd taken on three extra cleaning jobs, shifting her schedule around to fit them all in. By the time she got to Mr. Henning's house on Saturday, she had been exhausted. Fortunately, the bachelor was quite neat and there wasn't much to do at his place compared with the other houses, the ones with children. Mr. Henning was fastidious. She'd noticed he even threw out his birthday cards right away, not keeping them propped up on a table for weeks as she would. She found several cards on top of the kitchen trash, and another one in the basket near his desk. That one had been messy; tiny silver confetti sprinkled out when she opened it to see who it was from.

It was nice to think that Mr. Henning had a secret admirer. He should be married with a family of his own. After all, Mr. Henning had a good job. He worked at KEY

News, deciding which authors and books were featured on the network's morning program. Clara liked to watch *KEY to America* to see if she'd spot his name on the credits at the end of the show. But this morning's show was too depressing. All this talk about anthrax and weapons of mass destruction only made her feel worse.

She pushed herself up to turn off the television set but sank back against the pillow, her breathing labored. Clara worried about all the work she was missing as she sank into unconsciousness.

CHAPTER 4

As Annabelle approached the Broadcast Center, lights flashed from the large blue-and-white HAZMAT truck and the police squad cars that were parked at the curb. Annabelle flashed her KEY ID to get past the bright yellow police tape that cordoned off the sidewalk.

"Is it all right to go inside?" she asked the uniformed officer who guarded the heavy revolving door. Those hazardous-material guys with their bubble suits were intimidating.

"You go in at your own risk, lady, but we think it's all right. The studio is closed off while it's checked out. So is that clown Dr. Lee's office. Some doctor." He shook his head in disgust.

Annabelle could understand the cop's reaction. In fact, she shared it. She knew John Lee and was sure his motive for bringing that anthrax into the studio wasn't the altruistic one of informing the nation that weapons of mass destruction were available for the taking. Lee wanted the attention, the acclaim, the notoriety this stunt would bring. And from the look of things, he was getting his wish. Camera crews from ABC, CBS, NBC, and CNN were clustered on the sidewalk.

Taking a deep breath, Annabelle pushed through the revolving door.

The portable coffee-and-Danish trolley that was set up in the lobby each morning was strangely absent, and the hallways were quieter than usual. Had employees seen Lee's segment on the morning show and decided to stay home?

Annabelle took the elevator to the seventh floor, rehearsing what she would say to Yelena and Linus to convince them she had nothing to do with all this. Passing Jerome Henning's office on the way to her own, she stuck her head through the doorway, glad to see her friend was back after the two sick days he'd taken.

"Welcome back. Feeling better?" she asked.

"Somewhat," he answered, looking up from the press kit he was perusing and beckoning her to come inside.

"Close the door," he whispered.

Annabelle obeyed.

"Sit down for a minute," he instructed, shoving a stack of books aside on the couch to make a space for her.

"What's all the secrecy?" she asked, unbuttoning the top of her coat and throwing her gloves into her canvas tote bag.

"Did you know Lee was going to pull this, Annabelle?"

"Are you nuts? Of course, I didn't know. I wouldn't have the stomach for a stunt like this."

"Really?"

"Yeah, *really*." She emphasized the second word. "Come on, Jerome. You know me better than that. Lee had proposed a possible scenario at the morning meeting after he got back from his shoot at the lab. A 'what if' about stealing weapons-grade anthrax as proof that you can get it, and wanting to go on the air with it live, remember? You were there that morning."

Jerome nodded. "Yeah, and our beloved executive producer vetoed the idea. Lee wasn't very happy about that."

"Well, apparently Lee went ahead with his crazy plan anyway. But I knew nothing about it."

"Well that's good, because the Department of Health and the CDC are here, and the FBI are down the hall looking for you. They have some questions they want to ask you. I'll bet Yelena Gregory has some questions too." Jerome walked behind his cluttered desk and sat down while he waited for her to digest the information.

Annabelle closed her eyes and tilted her head back to rest against the top of the sofa. "Swell. That's just what I need right now," she groaned. "I can't decide which inquisitor frightens me more."

"Yelena, definitely." Jerome shrugged, and the corner of his mouth pulled downward. "Just tell them the truth. You didn't know what Lee was going to do. You don't know how he got ahold of the anthrax." He paused. "Right? You don't know how he got it." His voice trailed off, making the statement a question.

"Right, Jerome." She was adamant as she rose. "Look, I have nothing to hide. Nothing at all."

"I'm glad to hear it, Annabelle. Because this is going to be a mess." He pulled open the desk drawer and took out a white plastic bottle, snapping open the red lid.

"I thought you were feeling better," she said as she reached the door.

"I was, but I'm beginning to feel lousy again." He popped the Tylenol into his mouth. "I guess this flu is hanging on. I ache all over. I should have stayed home another day, but I have so much work to do. I've got to get through these and weed out the ones that aren't going to make it on the show." He gestured to the large containers of books that covered most of the office floor. "Speaking of which, did you get my last e-mail? Have you finished reading the manuscript? You've had the damned thing for two weeks. You're one of the best writers I know, Annabelle, and I value your opinion."

Annabelle grimaced in embarrassment. "It's right here, Jerome." She patted the tote bag. "I brought it home with me to finish last night, but I didn't get to it. You know, the kids and everything..."

"Yeah, yeah, I get it." He was clearly disappointed.

"I'm so sorry, Jerome. I want to read it, I really do, and I will. I promise."

"I understand. Your family has to come first."

Annabelle wanted to reach out and take hold of his arm, but she knew that probably wasn't a good idea. Instead, she suggested they have lunch together.

"Can I let you know later?" he asked. "I might go home after the meeting if I don't feel any better."

"Sure, but I have one thing to say, Jerome. You better be sure you have no desire to work at KEY News anymore because, from the bit I've read, if you publish this book, you'll never be welcome here again."

CHAPTER

5

In a locked examining room staffed by workers wearing respirator masks and nitrile gloves, every envelope, every package that came into the Broadcast Center was opened and inspected to make sure that neither anthrax nor any other dangerous substance made its way into the network news headquarters. But this danger had not been mailed in from the outside. It had been hand-delivered by one of KEY News's very own.

Security Director Joe Connelly was furious. Of all the lamebrain stunts, this one took the cake. And now he would have to pay the price, dealing with the New York City Police and Health Departments, the Centers for Disease Control, and the FBI. Not to mention the fears of the KEY employees that would need to be allayed.

That idiot Lee may have claimed that the container of anthrax had remained sealed, and there was a good chance that was true, but security demanded that they make no assumptions. The office and studio had to be closed off and tested to make sure none of the deadly spores had escaped. The NYPD "hammer team" was up there doing what needed to be done right now.

Joe scanned the dozens of video monitors along the wall of the security command post. Sixteen cameras on each chain were timed to record views of the various locations. Though not every inch of the Broadcast Center could be covered, cameras were trained on all entrances and exits, along hallways, outside each elevator. He spotted the grainy black-and-white images of the HAZMAT workers in the *KEY to America* studio; they looked like spacemen in their coveralls and helmets as they methodically took samples around the set.

Preliminary test results would be back in a few hours, though more accurate testing would take longer. But scores of people's lives would be disrupted and stressed today at a cost of who-knew-what for the police and health officials, the federal agents and lab testing, because Dr. John Lee had taken it upon himself to enlighten the public.

Thank you, thank you, Dr. Lee.

CHAPTER 6

Linus Nazareth leaned back in his chair and tossed his football into the air, catching it as it came spiraling downward. FBI Agents Leo McGillicuddy and Mary Lyons sat across from him, unamused.

"No, Special Agents, I didn't know. I had no idea that Dr. Lee was going to produce that vial of anthrax on the set this morning. But I can't say I am dismayed that he did. The public has a right to know the state of the nation's security on this." The atmosphere in the room was tense at the implicit accusation in the executive producer's statement.

Agent Lyons felt like smacking this obnoxious ass for the sneer in his voice when he said "Special Agents," but she kept her tone even. "We want to know how Dr. Lee got the anthrax. We want a detailed account of where and how Dr. Lee's story was produced, where he went, and who talked to him."

The football flew into the air again. "I don't have to give you that information and I won't."

"We're talking about a weapon of mass destruction here, Mr. Nazareth."

"That's your problem, not mine. Mine is protecting the public's right to know and making sure that my correspondents and producers can do their jobs. They can't do their jobs if they can't guarantee that they won't reveal their sources."

The agents looked at each other. Blah, blah, blah. They had heard this liberal jive before. It was clear that they weren't going to get anywhere with the arrogant jerk. They were wasting their time here. But there was more than one way to skin a cat.

They could get a tape of the broadcast and work backwards from there. Once they determined the lab where the story was taped, polygraph tests could be administered to the employees.

The post–September 11 cases at CBS, NBC, and ABC had been harder to solve; it had been next to impossible to trace the anthrax-laced missives among the millions and millions of letters that flowed through the U.S. mail. This time the chain of evidence should be much easier to follow.

CHAPTER 7

"Good, morning, Edgar. How are you today?" Annabelle smiled at the tall man pushing a stainless-steel service trolley down the carpeted hallway.

"Just fine, ma'am, I'm just fine. Thank you for asking."

In his starched white shirt, crisply pressed black trousers, and spit-polished shoes, Edgar took great pride in his appearance and in the Employee of the Month pin that he wore on his breast pocket. In his eight years of employment at KEY's Station Break cafeteria, he had never missed a day of work, always shown up for his shift when he was supposed to, many times even early. Edgar's supervisors loved him, and so did the *KEY to America* staffers as he delivered their coffee, bagels, and donuts each morning along with a warm, genuine smile.

We could all take a page from Edgar's book, thought Annabelle as she deposited her tote bag on her desk. He does his job well, with a quiet dignity, and he doesn't wear his troubles on his sleeve. Actually, she didn't know for certain if Edgar had troubles or not, but he couldn't be making a big salary and, for that reason alone, life in the New York metropolitan area had to be a struggle for him. But you'd never know it from the pleasant demeanor he always projected. There were those in the hallowed halls of the Broadcast Center who certainly made scads more money, enjoyed far more creature comforts, and would be considered much more "successful" than Edgar, yet they complained incessantly.

This thing has seen better days, she observed as she hung her navy wool coat on the hook on the back of her office door. Politically incorrect or not, tomorrow she was going to start wearing the fur jacket her aunt Florence had given her when she left for Florida. It had been hanging in the closet for years now, unworn. The poor animals had given their lives and pelts over fifteen years ago. The jacket would just have to do for now. Maybe after Christmas she could get something else on sale. Until then, the beaver jacket would keep her warm.

Annabelle picked up the telephone to retrieve her voicemail messages. She tensed as she heard Yelena Gregory's voice. "Annabelle. It's Yelena. Call me, immediately."

Taking a deep breath, Annabelle called the president's office. Yelena's assistant answered. "Yes, Annabelle. Yelena does want to talk with you, but she's in a meeting with the health department right now. Can you come to the office at ten forty-five?"

Of course she would come to the office. She had to let

Yelena know she had nothing to do with this. She had to keep her job.

Dr. John Lee's office door was closed but, through the window, Annabelle could see an orange-suited HAZMAT worker inside. Lee was in the screening room down the hall, talking on the telephone. He waved to her to come in. She didn't take a seat but stood, folding her arms across the yellow cashmere sweater Mike had splurged on two Christmases ago, as she waited.

"So let me get this straight." Lee scribbled across a yellow legal pad. "Either they will charge me with possession of a weapon of mass destruction or, more likely, they will haul me before a grand jury and try to make me tell where I got the stuff. And what happens if I refuse to talk?"

Annabelle watched as Lee listened to the response.

"And if the judge finds me in contempt, I go to jail until I give it up, right?" There was excitement but no worry in Lee's tone or facial expression. *He's actually enjoying this,* thought Annabelle with disbelief.

"Okay, Chris, call me after you talk to the federal prosecutor." Lee hung up the phone.

Until that moment, Annabelle hadn't been sure what tack she was going to take with her correspondent. Professionally, she was angry as hell that Lee had pulled this stunt without telling her. At the same time, she was glad she hadn't known anything about it. She could truthfully tell the FBI and Yelena as much, and only hope they believed her. She decided to stay calm, or at least appear calm, while inside she was seething.

"Your lawyer?" she asked.

"Yep. Christopher Neuman, one of the best in New York."

"You're gonna need him."

Lee shrugged and sat back in his chair. "I'm not particularly worried."

"That's interesting."

"Chris tells me that the prosecutor's office is probably not going to want to make a martyr out of me by prosecuting me. I'd be perceived as a brave journalist, doing my job by exposing the chinks in the armor of national security. They'll look bad if they prosecute a hero."

"So they'll go the grand jury route?"

Lee nodded. "Probably. And, of course, I'll refuse to reveal my sources," he declared smugly.

And you'll love the publicity generated by that, won't you? Ever the principled newsman. Just think how that will ratchet up your exposure and credibility as your agent negotiates your future contracts.

"And you're willing to go to jail?"

"If I have to, yes."

If she had thought for one minute that Dr. John Lee's motives were truly what he said they were, Annabelle would have admired him for his stance. But she knew him too well. Every fiber of her being told her that this was a calculated plan designed to help Lee get to his greater professional ambitions.

The idea of John Lee, M.D., behind bars wasn't all that upsetting as far as Annabelle was concerned.

CHAPTER 8

The group assembled around the conference table knew they were in for one of those meetings that would provide lots of material for later conversation at lunches and coffee breaks. As they sipped their java and picked at their corn muffins, the producers and correspondents waited for the executive producer, speculating on what Linus Nazareth's reaction would be to the events on this morning's show.

"I think it was deplorable," huffed Gavin Winston. "Lee had no right taking a risk like that. He should be fired immediately."

"I don't know, Gavin." Russ Parrish shrugged, twirling a strand of his curly, dark hair. "It sure was great television."

"You *would* think that," the business correspondent sniffed. "Everything has to have entertainment value to you."

"That's my job, Gavin, remember?"

Gavin tightened the knot of his silk tie. "Well, this isn't one of those movies you review, Russ. This is real life and anthrax is real stuff. Deadly stuff. Lee had one hell of a nerve. What do you think, Dominick?"

All eyes turned to the senior producer. Dominick O'Donnell was Nazareth's right-hand man.

"I, for one, am not particularly surprised, and I don't see why any of you are so shocked. When John floated his anthrax idea at the meeting last week, it must have crossed some minds here that he'd already obtained the anthrax from the lab."

No one at the conference table volunteered a response.

"Anyway," Dominick continued, "I think that the publicity on this is going to be great for ratings, and since we're in a sweeps period, Linus is going to be especially thrilled."

"The ratings, the ratings." Gavin's fist hit the table. "Damn the ratings."

"What sacrilege am I hearing?" Linus Nazareth stood in the doorway. The conference room fell instantly silent as the executive producer took his place at the table and fixed his gaze on the business correspondent.

"Come now, Gavin. Let's get off our high horse, shall we? Those ratings are what decide our advertising rates, and those ratings are what decide how much money we make, and that money, as you know, dear finance whiz, pays your extremely generous salary. So let's not pooh-pooh the importance of ratings. Remember, Gavin, winning isn't everything. It's the *only* thing."

Gavin's face colored while the others sat with eyes cast downward, suddenly immersed in the importance of their notes.

"Okay. Before we go any further, let me tell you that the anthrax container was completely sealed and there is no danger that any of the spores escaped. No one has to be worried about exposure. Having said that, if any of you want to get a prophylactic antibiotic, that's your prerogative. You can ask your doctor for a prescription for Cipro."

"Are you going to get some, Linus?" asked the weather forecaster, Caridad Vega.

"I have some that I stockpiled after the episodes at the other nets but, no, Carrie. I'm not going to take it. That's how confident I am that there is nothing to worry about here." Linus sat back in his chair and looked around the conference table, his expression defying anyone to question him further.

"All right," he continued, "now that we have that out of the way, I want you to know that, as of now, this broadcast and KEY News stand behind Dr. Lee and the public service he performed here. That is our official position. Personally, I did not know that John was going to do this, and I don't encourage any of you ever to make such an arbitrary decision. I must be informed of *every* important element of our broadcast. There are no exceptions to this rule."

"Except for Lee, I guess," Jerome Henning whispered to Annabelle.

Nazareth's eyes narrowed as he focused on the book segment producer. "Do you have something to say, Jerome?"

"Sorry, Linus. I was just telling Annabelle how lousy I feel."

"I see. Well, why don't you go first this morning so we can let you out of here and spare us the golden opportunity of catching whatever you've got?"

Trying to ignore the comment, Jerome rattled off the list of authors who would be available for the remainder of the week, giving quick synopses of the books they were promoting. The last on the list was a much-anticipated tell-all written by the mistress of a well-known politician.

"Who's the publisher on that one?" asked Nazareth.

"Ephesus." Jerome coughed.

Nazareth nodded. "Good. Book it."

Jerome didn't bother to mention that he already had. Ephesus was publishing Linus Nazareth's book as well, and Jerome knew that the "coach" might want to keep his publisher happy. The publishing company had paid a handsome advance for an insider's view of the top-rated morning show written by the flamboyant broadcasting executive with the agreement that Linus Nazareth write every word himself.

But Linus had quickly realized it wasn't so easy to pump out a book. It took a patience he did not have, and he had turned to Jerome for help with *The "Only" Thing: Winning the TV News Game.*

With carefully concealed contempt, Jerome watched as the executive producer turned his embarrassing vitriol on his next victim. After writing all that self-aggrandizing claptrap for Linus, Jerome had seen his chance to set the record straight by telling the real story and, at the same time, claiming some fame and fortune for himself. He may have signed a confidentiality agreement swearing not to reveal that he had ghostwritten his boss's book, but nothing said he couldn't write one of his own.

When his own manuscript was sold and published, Jerome knew he'd have burned his bridges. But he planned to get in a stinging parting shot. In his mind, he'd already fashioned the dedication.

For "Coach" Nazareth . . .

If not for you, I wouldn't have had the impetus to write this.

CHAPTER 9

It was surprising that Jerome was still up and functioning. Those nasty little bacteria were no doubt multiplying in his lungs, pushing him, though he did not know it, to the inevitable. Since this would surely be the last time they'd see each other, it was irresistible to get in a few choice words. Not too much could be revealed, no threats or confessions that would spur Jerome to look for help. Just a few words to let him know that his actions had consequences.

Jerome was in his office, pulling on his jacket and getting ready to leave, when the knock came on the open door. With tiny beads of perspiration glistening on his forehead and his face flushed, he was looking really bad. In a pained voice, he apologized. "I'm so sorry, but can this possibly wait? I feel awful and I've got to get out of here. The car service is waiting downstairs to take me home."

"Don't worry. I'll be quick. I just wanted you to know, Jerome, that I don't appreciate that you intended to tell the world about us."

"What are you talking about?"

"I read your enterprising little masterpiece. I had no idea you were so vicious, Jerome."

"I don't know what you're talking about and I can't really talk now. I have to get home and get to bed."

"You should have told Annabelle to be more careful with it. She left your manuscript in her office."

Jerome was incredulous. "May I ask what you were doing snooping around in Annabelle's office?"

"That's neither here nor there. I won't have this turned around on me, making me feel like the criminal, when what you have done is so reprehensible. You should be ashamed of yourself."

Jerome stalked past. "Well, I'm not, particularly. Now get away from the door, please, so I can lock it. I'm going home."

CHAPTER 10

Lauren Adams stood on the crowded sidewalk, staring down at her new Prada boots. Though they had cost her almost a week's take-home pay, she rationalized that the boots were a good investment, a statement. Anyone worthwhile would recognize the soft leather and fine stitching and make the assumption she wanted them to make. She was a person of quality, someone to be taken seriously.

As she waited for her cameraman to drive the car up from the garage, Lauren watched another police car pull up, and the video crews from the other networks record the latest in the situation at KEY News.

The wind blew, and she brushed her long dark hair back from her face. She was glad she hadn't missed the staff meeting this morning. She always enjoyed the after-show postmortems Linus conducted. *KEY to America* correspondents and producers gathered in the conference room to listen to the executive producer's views on what had pleased him on the just-aired broadcast and his tirades on what hadn't. Since Linus never took his wrath out on her, she usually had a fine time. In fact, some of the best time she and Linus spent together was right after the meeting. He was so exhilarated then.

This morning's meeting had been an especially good show.

The dark gray sedan pulled up to the curb, and Lauren got in, mentally cringing as her alpaca coat pressed against the coffee-stained seat.

"Where to?" asked B.J. D'Elia, bracing himself for the hours to come with the prima donna.

Lauren rattled off the address of the uptown psychologist's office. It had been hard to get this interview, and she needed it for the series she was preparing on educational toys. Erector sets, puzzles, pocket microscopes, reflector telescopes, and levitating globes were predicted to be big sellers this Christmas season. Lauren needed a sound bite or two from the fancy-schmancy child analyst on the benefits of these types of toys.

She took out a reporter's notebook from her Hermès bag and made a note to call the chemistry-set manufacturer and ask them to send another one over. The first promotional one they'd provided was gone.

CHAPTER 11

White powder. White powder. White powder.

With all the talk this morning about anthrax, Russ Parrish could focus only on the other white powder. The one he craved.

He wished he had never tried cocaine. He'd always heard that the feeling it produced was so fantastic it was nearly impossible to avoid getting hooked. Somehow, he'd thought it wouldn't happen to him. He would be one of the few who could control himself.

He should have known better. Occasional recreational use had turned into addiction. There was no use sugarcoating it. He was hooked, and his was an expensive passion.

Russ closed his door, glad again that he had one of the inside offices, lacking windows. Others might complain about the sunless boxes to which they'd been assigned at the Broadcast Center, the gigantic dairy which had been converted into KEY headquarters, but Russ's space suited him just fine. He could have his privacy when he wanted and needed it.

He pulled his wallet from his pocket and took out a credit card, a crisp twenty-dollar bill, and a small, precisely folded paper envelope. Carefully opening the envelope, Russ tapped the powder down into the crease. Using his desk as his workspace, he took the edge of the credit card and rhythmically chopped at the cocaine, dissolving the tiny clumps that had formed. When he was satisfied that the powder was all the same consistency, Russ rolled the twenty-dollar bill into a thin tube and placed it against his nostril. As he bent his head down to the desktop, the currency tube became the delivery chute through which he snorted the white powder.

He caught a glimpse of himself in the mirror that hung on the wall opposite his desk. He watched, loathing himself, as his eyes began to water and his face reddened. He shot his cuff out from beneath his soft leather jacket and raised the back of his hand to wipe at his nose. Disgusting behavior, but man, the feeling that was coming over him was great.

It was almost a cliché, wasn't it? The entertainment reporter hooked right along with the Hollywood stars and music giants who had gotten in too deep. Sex, drugs, and rock 'n' roll. Life in the fast lane.

CHAPTER 12

He could tell the sweet young thing was uncomfortable, but Gavin pushed on anyway. After Linus's tongue-lashing at the morning meeting, the veteran business correspondent needed something to make himself feel better, bigger, more important. The pretty intern with her unlined face, tight sweater, and short skirt was just the ticket to massage his wounded ego.

The college students worked for free just to spend time at a major broadcasting network. Sometimes the necessary connections were made to help with getting a job at KEY after graduation. At the very least the students walked away with an impressive credential to list on their résumés.

The interns were bright-eyed and eager and easily impressed. Gavin looked forward to the new crop of females who started working each semester. Lily was the pick of this fall's litter.

Long blond hair, with wispy bangs that fell into her big, soft brown eyes. Bambi-esque, Lily's eyes were. Innocent and trusting, so unlike the steely, dark eyes of Marguerite, his shrewish wife.

Resolutely, Gavin pushed from his mind the thought of the woman he had been chained to for a quarter of a century and continued making conversation with Lily.

"I was thinking that you might want to come with me this afternoon for an interview I have to do down at the NASDAQ," he offered. "It would be good experience for you to get out of the building and see some field reporting."

"Gee, thank you, Mr. Winston, that would be great. I really appreciate you doing that for me."

"Call me Gavin, dear. Mr. Winston makes me feel like I could be your father." He chuckled.

The intern laughed nervously. *My father is younger than you are,* she thought.

CHAPTER 13

In the time she had between the morning meeting and her appointment with Yelena, Annabelle quickly went through her e-mails, deleting another one of Jerome's pleas that she finish reading his manuscript, and then she called home. The phone rang again and again until, finally, Mike answered.

"I was just about to hang up, honey," Annabelle said, trying to keep the concern out of her voice. "Where were you?"

"Lying down."

Her heart sank. Mike was sleeping away yet another day. In all the years they'd been together, Annabelle had never known him even to take a nap on a Sunday afternoon. A day off from the firehouse meant he was really physically ill, and those days were exceedingly rare. Now, day after day, week after week, Mike's hours were spent alone in the apartment, lying in bed with the shades pulled down, alternately sleeping and thrashing dark thoughts over and over in his mind.

Even the twins couldn't pull him out of his misery. Mrs.

Nuzzo told her that Tara and Thomas had stopped trying to go in and talk to him when she brought them home from school each afternoon. The children had been rebuffed too many times. Instead, they stayed with their baby-sitter until Mommy came home from work, waiting to tell their other parent how their day at school had gone.

"Did you get the kids to school all right?"

"Yeah, the poor things were actually excited that I was taking them."

"They love you, Mike." She was tempted to add, "And they're worried about you," but she didn't want her husband to feel worse than he already did. Editing herself was a way of life now, choosing her words carefully so as not to upset him. She ached for the not-so-long-ago days when they could say anything to each other.

"How's work?"

He was interested? A hopeful sign.

"Not great. I'm about to go into a meeting with Yelena Gregory and the rest to get raked over the coals for this anthrax thing."

"What anthrax thing?"

Her hopes were dashed.

"Remember? I told you about it this morning before I rushed to work? That's why you had to walk the twins to school."

"Oh, yeah," he answered dully. "Well, I'm sure you'll work things out. KEY News is lucky to have you, Annabelle."

"I'm glad you think so, honey," she answered, feeling very alone. "After this morning, I hope they do."

Annabelle took a quick look around the president's office. She had never been in here before, and she had somehow expected something more. Television monitors, each tuned to a different network, were mounted on the bookcase behind Yelena Gregory's massive desk. Framed journalism awards decorated the dove gray walls, and an Oriental rug covered the floor. But the room wasn't especially large, nor was the view out the windows particularly impressive. Snarled traffic on Fifty-seventh Street.

Security Chief Joe Connelly sat in one of the chairs across from Yelena's desk; Linus Nazareth was in another. Feeling like an errant schoolgirl called down to the principal's office, Annabelle took a place next to John Lee on the sofa.

"Let's get right to it," Yelena snapped. "I want to know how this happened."

All eyes went to Linus, but he was looking at John Lee. The force of the stare directed the others to turn in the direction of the sofa.

"Yelena"—Lee squirmed—"I realize now that I shouldn't have unilaterally decided to do what I did, but I was afraid if

I told anyone I had gotten the anthrax and was planning to bring it on the broadcast, the plan might have gotten the kibosh."

"So you took it on yourself to make this decision? Without discussing it with your producer or running it by the executive producer?" Yelena asked with skepticism.

Annabelle felt the heat rise on her cheeks as the room waited for Lee's answer.

"Yes. I did it all on my own. And in my defense, it was a story worth telling. America needs to know."

Yelena's eyes narrowed. "Be that as it may, you had no right to go on air with something of this magnitude without running it by anyone up the chain of command. Now, for legal and reputation reasons, KEY News is put in the position of having to defend you and your actions, and I resent it. If we had known what you were planning to do and gave the green light on it, we could have been prepared with a response. Now we're scrambling with damage control. Personally, I could wring your neck, John."

Annabelle thought she actually heard a tiny whimper alongside her. She couldn't stand this guy, but she took no pleasure in watching him get skewered.

Linus jumped in. "You're right, Yelena. We have to decide how to go on from here. I've already told the FBI that we don't have to tell them anything."

"And my lawyer says the feds won't prosecute because it

will make them look bad," Lee interjected with hope. "They don't want to be seen as beating up on a journalist who was only exposing a public danger."

"Is that how you see yourself, John? A brave journalist whose sole aim was to protect the public?" The sarcasm in Yelena's voice was cutting as she rose from her desk and walked to the window. "Funny, but I think that your own ambitions had a little something to do with this."

He should have kept his mouth shut, thought Annabelle. She was more determined than ever to speak only when asked.

Again, Linus interrupted. "Let's face it, Yelena. Ambition is the name of the game. I can't think of any reporter worth his salt who doesn't want to be on the air, telling his story. That's what a reporter does, that's what he works for and fights for. KEY News is not going to look bad in this thing, Yelena. We look like heroes, telling the public what they need to know. That's how we play this." He pounded his hand on the arm of the chair for emphasis. "And though it's the dirty little secret, that's how we get ratings."

With the light streaming in from the window behind her, Yelena's large frame loomed. The others in the room waited for her to speak.

"Believe it or not, I'm not all that worried about ratings right now, Linus. My instinct is to can John. But, at the moment, I can't. I think it's best to stand beside him for the time being. But, believe me, it's an uneasy alliance."

CHAPTER 14

By the time the car pulled out on the New Jersey side of the Lincoln Tunnel, Jerome Henning had given the driver a new destination.

"Essex Hills Hospital, in Maplewood, please." He then suggested they go west on Route 280, glad that he'd hired the car service. There was no way he could deal with taking his usual train to the suburbs.

It was getting harder to breathe, his chest was so tight. This didn't feel like any flu or virus he'd ever had before. He had to get to a doctor, but since he had no personal physician, the emergency room of the hospital nearest his home was probably the best option. Maybe he should have gone straight to a New York City hospital. People always seemed to assume that those were superior to the ones in Jersey. He should have asked Annabelle what she thought.

He pulled his cell phone from his pocket, having to muster unusual concentration to think of the number and push the buttons on the keypad. The phone rang five times before transferring to the answering message.

"Hi. This is Annabelle Murphy, medical producer for *KEY to America.* I'm either on another line or away from my desk, so please leave your name, number, and the time that you called and I'll get back to you as soon as I can. Or you can try me on my cell phone." Annabelle's recorded voice recited the number.

After the beep, Jerome managed to speak. "Annabelle, I'm on my way home, to Essex Hills Hospital, actually. I was going to ask you what you thought about it, but I guess the Jersey docs can fix me up. Sorry I couldn't make our lunch today. I still want to hear what you think about the book. I'll try to call you later."

He was snapping the phone closed when he remembered he had wanted to warn Annabelle about the unlikely office snoop and chide her for leaving the manuscript out where someone could read it, but he hadn't the energy to call back on either her cell phone or her office line.

CHAPTER

15

"Do you think we should have nasal swabs taken?"

Wayne Nazareth was waiting for Annabelle when she returned from Yelena's office. If he paced up and down much longer he would wear a hole in the carpet, thought Annabelle. She felt sorry for the thin, intense young man. It was bad enough having Linus Nazareth as a boss. Annabelle couldn't imagine having him as a father. Wayne was as quiet as his father was brash. Thoughtful and talented, yet well aware of the whispers of nepotism that hissed through the office.

"I'm not going to, Wayne," she answered. "The nose is the body's first line of defense. There are thousands of germs swirling around in there, and even if anthrax is in the nose, that doesn't mean it's in the lungs. Besides, the container of anthrax was sealed. We haven't been exposed."

"Then why were those HAZMAT guys in the orange suits wearing boots and masks when they checked the studio and Lee's office?"

"Taking precautions, I would imagine, while they tested.

But Lee says he never opened the anthrax, and I believe him. He may be many things, but he's not suicidal."

Wayne considered Annabelle's reasoning. He didn't want to be a wimp, but he was worried. "I don't know," he said, his brow furrowed.

"Look, Wayne, if it will make you feel better, get tested. But just know that while those nasal swabs may allay public fear, they're not very useful at a clinical level. If it comes up positive, all it means is you've been exposed. That doesn't necessarily translate into an infection."

"Then maybe I should just get a prescription for Cipro?" he grasped.

Annabelle tried to be patient. "Again, I wouldn't, Wayne. That's an antibiotic that you'll have to take for sixty days. It causes serious side effects for some people. And even more important, if you take antibiotics when you don't really need them, there's a chance they won't work if and when you do."

Annabelle didn't know what else she could say to assuage the young man's fears. She decided to try to distract him. "If you don't have another assignment, I could use some help with my story. I have to do the follow-up on this thing."

"Gee, Annabelle, I'd like to help you out, I really would, but I already have a load of stuff I'm working on. I have to go down to Wall Street and do an interview for Gavin, and I promised Lauren I'd do some research and pull file tape for her piece." He backed out the door.

Watching him disappear down the hall, Annabelle wondered what it would be like to have a brother, a twin no less, lying for twenty years in a vegetative state, a sibling you had been with since conception, as close as two people could be. She thought of Thomas and Tara, and the special bond between them. Chilled, she rubbed her arms, imagining what it would be like for one of them to watch the other sink beneath the broken ice of a skating pond, as Jerome's manuscript recounted six-year-old Wayne Nazareth had done all those years ago. According to Jerome's research, Wayne had stood there, screaming for help, not wanting to run away from his brother. How had he dealt with the realization, which must have come as he grew older, that those precious wasted minutes could have made a difference? If he had gone for help right away, his brother might have been all right. It was too horrible to dwell on, and she intended to tell Jerome that, in her opinion, he should strike that chapter from his secret manuscript.

It was too cruel.

CHAPTER 16

Joe Connelly returned to the president's office with the latest news.

"The FBI want to see John Lee's e-mails," he announced.

From behind her desk, Yelena looked up without expression. "What a surprise."

"What do you say? Should we cooperate?" the security chief asked.

"No, Joe. If the feds want Lee's e-mails, let them get a subpoena."

CHAPTER 17

Today was definitely a day to lunch at Michael's, but not because of the California-sunny decor or the mouthwatering menu. The restaurant was a media hangout, known for the power lunching that went on within its spacious layout.

The *KEY to America* executive producer and his lunch companion were shown to a table near the front of the room. Linus enjoyed being up front. This way everyone who entered or exited the restaurant had to pass by, nodding acknowledgment or stopping to exchange pleasantries. They had arrived later than usual today, but there still were enough diners willing to pay homage.

"Helluva job with that anthrax story this morning, Linus."

"Way to go, buddy. That was damn fine television."

"Congratulations to both of you. You really provided a public service."

Linus basked in the praise as the salads arrived at the table.

"You see, John? You're a hero. Maybe these guys didn't know who you were before, but you've made a name for yourself now."

Lee took a sip from his wineglass. "I'm not feeling like a hero after that meeting with Yelena."

"Don't worry about Yelena. She'll come around when she sees that this was all good for KEY News."

"I'd feel better if you told her the truth, Linus."

The executive producer frowned. "Hey, we agreed, didn't we? I had to veto the plan in front of her at the meeting. If I had gone to Yelena ahead of time and told her what we were going to do, there was no guarantee she would have gone for it. It was good for the show and good for your career, and that's all we have to concern ourselves with."

"Still, I wish you would have told her that you knew about everything beforehand."

If wishes were horses, beggars would ride. The old adage flew through Linus's mind. No, he was glad everything had played out exactly as he had planned.

Linus speared a piece of blackened chicken with his fork. "Let's not send each other any more e-mails on this subject, John. We can't be too careful. From now on, we'll only talk about this face-to-face."

CHAPTER 18

The emergency room doctor placed his stethoscope on Jerome's back. "Deep breath," he commanded.

The intake of air collapsed into repetitive coughing.

"Do you have a runny nose?"

Jerome shook his head groggily. "No. Just the fever and the body- and headaches, and now I'm having trouble breathing. And I'm very, very tired."

"Okay, we're going to get a blood test done and do a chest X ray."

This wasn't a common cold gone bad.

"What do you do for a living, Mr. Henning?" the doctor asked as he made notations on his chart.

"I'm a producer at KEY News, on *KEY to America*."

"Really? I watch the show almost every morning."

"I do the book segments."

"Interesting."

The doctor's mind was not on the latest best-seller being

hawked. It was on this morning's anthrax story, which everyone was talking about.

After September 11, he had done extensive reading on biological and chemical agents, but this couldn't be happening right before his eyes, could it?

CHAPTER 19

The FBI was finally getting around to questioning her.

"I feel like I should have a lawyer or something," Annabelle said as she indicated that the agents should take a seat.

"That's your prerogative, of course," answered the female agent, "but you aren't being accused of anything here. We just have some general questions we'd like to ask you."

"All right."

"You were the producer of Dr. Lee's piece this morning, correct?"

"Yes, that's right."

"And we've been told that you knew nothing of Dr. Lee's

intention to obtain anthrax and bring it into this building. Is that also correct?"

"Yes, it is. He had talked once about the idea, but I never thought he would actually do it, especially after Linus Nazareth told him not to."

"When did Nazareth say that?"

"At a staff meeting one morning last week."

The FBI agent made a notation.

"Do you have any idea how he got the anthrax?"

Annabelle paused before answering. "I would imagine he obtained it from the lab where part of the piece was shot, but I don't know for sure."

"Were you with Dr. Lee at the lab?"

For once, Annabelle was glad that KEY News was under such strict budget constrictions. Beth Terry, the unit manager, had approved the travel expenses for only the medical correspondent to fly out to the lab. Annabelle had set up the lab shoot and arranged for a local camera crew over the telephone but hadn't actually flown to the site.

"No, I wasn't."

"So you don't know who Dr. Lee may have had contact with once he was at the lab?"

"That's correct."

As the agents were rising to leave, Annabelle glanced at her computer screen and clicked on the message directed to all personnel. Yelena Gregory was going to do a closed-circuit broadcast to the employees to announce the good news. Preliminary tests showed no trace of anthrax in the Broadcast Center. With a sigh of relief, Annabelle checked her phone messages, learned that she would be lunching alone, and headed for the cafeteria.

CHAPTER 20

Usually, it was hard to go anywhere without being noticed. But today staffers were paying more attention to the hazardous-material personnel milling about and less to people they saw all the time. At lunchtime it wasn't difficult to slip into Annabelle's office and shut the door. Standing right behind the closed door ensured no detection from the window to the hallway.

Just a minute. That was all the time that was needed.

The protective gloves were pulled over quivering hands. *Steady. Steady.*

If anyone walked in, there was an explanation all planned.

Annabelle had lent a few dollars to a colleague when the

downstairs ATM machine was broken, and now the money was being repaid. That was, after all, true. The money had been loaned, and now it was being tucked in the pocket of the worn navy wool coat that hung on the back of Annabelle's door. A twenty-dollar bill along with a tissue coated with the finest dusting of white powder. Annabelle would surely use it.

It was cold outside, and runny noses were the norm.

CHAPTER 21

The afternoon mail had brought quite a nice haul. Four new CDs from the music companies, three DVDs of major movies that were being released at Christmastime, and two computer games, all sent to the *KEY to America* entertainment correspondent in hopes of getting some free publicity on the morning show.

Russ stuffed the CDs and DVDs in his attaché case and tossed the computer games aside. He had no desire to play around on the computer. His time was much too valuable for that. He had concerts and Broadway shows to enjoy, cocktail parties and galas to attend. Better for him to rub elbows with actors, directors, and the titans of the entertainment industry at movie openings than while away the hours clicking on a computer mouse at home.

Russ ran a hand through his dark, curly hair. He'd knock off work early this afternoon so that he could pick up his dinner jacket at the dry cleaner's and stop for a haircut on the way home to change for tonight's affair, a movie screening followed by a party at the Copacabana. Free eats and drinks and a chance to do some networking and score some coke. What could be bad? With a little luck, he would be out of there by ten o'clock.

He was a guest of the producers of *Icicle,* the soon-to-be-released flick that had cost multimillions to make but, from the clip he had already seen, was destined to be a flop. Russ knew that the invitation was an attempt to persuade him to go easy on his review.

It would take more than dinner and drinks to make that happen.

CHAPTER 22

The white blood cell count was high, and there was no increase in lymphocytes. People with infections such as the flu usually had low white blood cell counts and increased lymphocyte counts. That, along with the abnormalities in the chest X ray, had the doctor worried.

"Mr. Henning, we're going to do a CT scan and a blood culture."

"Jesus, Doc, you're scaring me," Jerome whispered as he lay in the hospital bed. The discomfort in his chest was getting worse.

"Don't worry, Mr. Henning. We're going to get you started on an antibiotic to knock whatever it is out of your system."

Out in the hallway, the doctor instructed the nurse. "Let's get him started on ciprofloxacin."

"Cipro?"

The doctor nodded. "Normally, the odds are one in three hundred million that this could be anthrax. But I'm not taking any chances."

He had to call the health department.

CHAPTER

23

What a day he'd had. Suffering through Lauren Adams most of the day only to be followed by Gavin Winston. B.J. couldn't wait to finish shooting this interview, pack up his camera gear, and get the hell home.

It was distasteful to watch, really. While waiting for the official to arrive in the NASDAQ interview area, Gavin was working hard to impress that little intern. The poor kid didn't know what to do. She was trying to be polite, laughing at the geezer's pathetic attempts at humor, attempting to ignore the innuendos the old coot tossed her way. B.J. had half a mind to report Gavin's behavior to Yelena Gregory.

Finally, the financial spokesman arrived, cutting short for the moment Gavin's macho performance. The business correspondent instantly and artfully switched gears, asking professional, well-informed questions about the state of the stock market and the outlook for technology stocks. The guy may be a lech, but B.J. had to give credit where credit was due. Gavin knew his stuff.

The interview took all of ten minutes. As B.J. broke down his lights and started wrapping up the extension wires, he pretended not to hear Gavin ask the intern out for a drink.

"Gee, I'm sorry, Mr. Winston, but I can't. I already have plans," answered the young woman.

Gavin was undeterred. "Just a quick one, Lily. I'd like to talk to you about your career plans. And it's Gavin, remember?"

CHAPTER 24

It was a nuisance more than anything else. The U.S. attorney had easily obtained the subpoena for access to Dr. Lee's e-mails.

Special Agent McGillicuddy read through the hard copies.

"Well, we already knew that Linus Nazareth is an ass; now we know that he's a liar too," he said, passing the message to his partner. "A smart liar, though, covering himself by denouncing Lee's plan in front of everyone at that staff meeting."

Agent Lyons read the correspondence between Lee and

Nazareth, which confirmed that both parties had planned the anthrax episode.

"Think we should tell Yelena Gregory and Joe Connelly?" Lyons asked.

Still annoyed that he'd had to bother with getting a subpoena, McGillicuddy was in no mood to share anything with the news folks. He shook his head and frowned. "No. Let them figure it out for themselves."

CHAPTER 25

Relieving Mrs. Nuzzo, Annabelle arrived home with a pizza box in her hands. The kids were thrilled with the prospect of a gooey tomato-and-cheese dinner, but she guiltily peeled some carrots and sliced some celery sticks in an attempt to construct the semblance of a well-balanced meal.

"How was school today?" she asked as she poured the milk.

"Can't we have ginger ale, Mommy?" implored Thomas.

"No, you can't have ginger ale."

"Ginger ale goes better with pizza," declared Tara.

"Yeah, it does," her brother seconded.

"Yes, it does," corrected Annabelle. "But you have to have milk with your dinner."

"The Pilgrims didn't have milk with their dinner," said Tara. "They had apple cider."

"Well, you can be a Pilgrim next week. We'll have apple cider on Thanksgiving. But if you want to go horseback riding on Saturday, you're having milk tonight."

Thanksgiving was a week away, and Annabelle dreamed of having the dinner delivered from Zabar's. The thought of doing the shopping and all that cooking for just the four of them was a downer. Maybe she could make a streamlined Thanksgiving dinner this year, cook a turkey breast instead of a whole bird, do an instant stuffing, and open a can of cranberry sauce. As long as she made lots of mashed potatoes, the kids would be satisfied and, at this point, Mike certainly didn't care. He rarely ate dinner with them anymore, preferring to close the door to the bedroom and lie on the bed, either in the dark or staring morosely at the portable television set.

She listened to Tara list the things that they were going to have at their classroom Thanksgiving feast. "We have to bring in pumpkin pie, Mommy."

Good. That was easy enough. She could pick one up at the grocery store.

"We're supposed to help you make it," said Thomas.

Okay, a Mrs. Smith's then. Together, they could open the box and stick the frozen pie in the oven.

While the kids were finishing up, Annabelle went to the bedroom. The room was dark.

"Mike?" she called softly.

No answer.

"Do you want some pizza, honey?"

Nothing.

Biting her lower lip to keep from screaming in frustration, she closed the bedroom door and walked to the bathroom. She turned the faucet on full force, squirted in the Mr. Bubble, and stared as the white froth spread across the tub. The baths had to be given, the teeth brushed, and the stories read. She hoped she could get to bed early herself, as she wanted to be at work by 6:00 A.M., in case there was anything to do for Dr. Lee's interview on the show. If there was no other breaking news, Linus wanted Lee to lead the broadcast.

If she'd been assigned to one of the other correspondents, her workload would have been lighter. The good ones prided themselves on knowing their subject matter and doing their own writing. But Lee only loved being on television while leaving all the work that went on behind the scenes to Annabelle.

She suddenly remembered that she must call Jerome to see how he was doing. She should have done that hours ago. Great friend she was.

While the tub filled, she went out to the kitchen, pulled her cell phone from her tote bag, and punched in Jerome's number.

The electronic ring of the cell phone was muffled in the pocket of the jacket that hung in the small closet of the hospital room. Outside, the doctor and nurses did what they had to, connecting Jerome to a ventilator.

CHAPTER 26

Maybe a commuter pass was in order. This was the second train ride in less than a week out to Maplewood.

Annabelle could be thanked for spreading the word around the office that Jerome was sick enough to go to the hospital, and a phone call confirmed he had been admitted. The green light for another trip to New Jersey. It had to be done tonight or it would be too late. Once the hospital figured out what was wrong with Jerome, the health department and the police would be called in, and surely Jerome's house would be searched.

The path from the station to Highland Place was now a

familiar one. The streets were quiet, and none of the few people passing by paid any attention to the visitor. Walking with assurance, as if belonging there, the visitor went around to the back of the unlit house. The first window was locked, but the second one slid right open.

Trusting fools, these suburbanites.

It was a struggle to get through the ground-floor window. The mask and gloves were donned as a precautionary measure. Though the tube in the coat pocket was carefully wrapped, there was no way of knowing exactly where Jerome had opened his cheery birthday card.

The flashlight cast its yellow glow around the kitchen, then into the dining room and through the living room. The beam led the way up the stairs to the small bedroom that served as an office. A computer sat amid the clutter on the desk. After it was switched on, it took only a few minutes to find the right file and just a little while longer to erase it. All that work, pages and pages of manuscript, obliterated with just the tapping of the Delete key.

Jerome must have printed out a hard copy as well—there it was in the top desk drawer. The folder was taken from its berth and replaced with the test tube.

The police would find the anthrax and think that Jerome had exposed himself.

How was anyone to know that a bit of the tube's contents had been put aside just in case it was needed? You need so little to do so much damage.

FRIDAY

— NOVEMBER 21 —

CHAPTER 27

Joe Connelly spent the night in one of the soap opera dressing rooms, wanting to be nearby if the worst-case scenario played out and the preliminary tests were wrong. If it turned out that anthrax had contaminated any part of the Broadcast Center, he needed to be there to deal with it.

After a night of restless half-sleep, he took a quick shower in the tiny bathroom, dressed in the fresh shirt and underwear he kept in his office for emergencies, and stopped in the cafeteria for a hot cup of coffee to carry back with him to the security command post.

Station Break was quiet at this early hour, but Edgar was already at work, stocking the coffee trolley.

"Mornin'." The food service worker smiled.

"Good morning, Edgar. How's it going?"

"Fine, sir. Just fine."

"Glad to hear it."

He watched the security boss stop to leave money at the register, as the cashier wasn't in yet.

An honest person.

But they weren't all like that. Some people thought it was fine to take tea bags, cereal, soda, juice—even cheese, right off the salad bar—without bothering to pay. Last week, someone he couldn't believe had actually gone right into the kitchen and poured out a cup of powdered sugar. Edgar had pretended, as he always did, not to notice.

And he didn't want any trouble.

CHAPTER 28

Annabelle preferred to take the subway to work but, at this early hour, a taxi seemed safer and a lot more convenient, even if it was more expensive.

It was still dark when her cab pulled up in front of the Broadcast Center. She paid the driver and got out just as a blue Lincoln Town Car slid to the curb. Annabelle knew that one of the *KTA* hosts would be in the backseat. The hired cars that brought them to work at this ungodly hour came with the jobs. She was delighted to see it was Constance

Young rather than Harry Granger stepping from the rear door of the car.

"Am I glad to see you," Annabelle said, bussing her friend on the cheek.

Constance gave Annabelle a hug, her hand petting the plush brown fur that covered Annabelle's arm.

"New jacket, huh?" she observed, squinting in the dim light that streamed from the lobby windows onto the sidewalk.

"Don't even go there—I'm waiting for the animal rights activists to spray me with red paint any minute," said Annabelle. "And it's not new. It's fifteen years old. Let's call it 'vintage,' shall we?"

The two pushed through the revolving door and swiped their ID cards across the electronic scanner. In the lobby light, Annabelle marveled at how beautiful Constance was even without her makeup. Her alabaster skin was flawless.

"I missed you yesterday. How was your trip?"

"Good," Constance affirmed. "The shoot went well, and I was even able to squeeze in a late lunch with my old boss at the Boston affiliate. But I've got to tell you, I hated leaving right after the show to fly up there. What did I miss?"

Annabelle filled her in on the interview with the FBI and the meeting with Yelena. "Our president is not a happy camper, Constance. I sure wouldn't want to be in John Lee's shoes right now." She frowned. "Come to think of it, I wouldn't want to be in Yelena Gregory's either."

CHAPTER 29

Her muscles aching with tension, Yelena stood beneath the shower spray and let the needles of hot water pound against her ample body. It would be nice if she could closet herself in the shower stall all day, she thought, but there was too much to do, starting with watching *KTA* from the very beginning this morning.

She turned off the water and forced herself from the shower. Standing on the soft white bath mat, she dried herself off, still careful when she came to the old hysterectomy scar, the symbol of the children she was never meant to have. Yelena had always thought there was going to be time to have children, once she got her career on track, once she met the right man. But the career had become all-consuming, the hours long, her time dictated by the unpredictable turns of breaking news. The men she had met found it difficult to play second fiddle to her work. They didn't like having plans canceled because news happened, forcing her into the office. And as she rose in the news hierarchy, the only men Yelena seemed to come in contact with were the ones she worked with. Her one foray with an office romance had been disastrous. Pete Carlson had only used her to help his own career goals. She still hadn't recovered emotionally from that fiasco.

As she looked in the mirror and applied moisturizer to her face, Yelena was all too aware that the years had slipped by, good years, productive years, sometimes exciting years, but years filled with memories of KEY News—not of a fulfilling personal life. At fifty-three, she knew with certainty there would be no children or grandchildren, and she seriously doubted that she would ever get married. But that was all right, she told herself, because she had KEY News. KEY News was her baby. KEY News was the child she cared for with all of her intellect and passion.

And now, her baby was threatened. With its reputation on the line, Yelena was determined to do anything she could to ensure that KEY News kept its place of honor in the broadcasting world. Absolutely nothing mattered to her more.

The organization was only as good as the people who staffed it, and KEY had many intelligent and creative minds working in its offices around the world. Yelena paid careful attention to the people she hired, searching out the most talented individuals and luring them into the ranks of her news force. The *KEY Evening Headlines with Eliza Blake* was progressing nicely in the ratings—no small feat against the likes of Rather, Jennings, and Brokaw. *Hourglass,* with Cassie Sheridan, after major contract negotiations, finally in the newsmagazine anchor chair, led its prime-time hour slot. And *KEY to America* was blowing away the morning competition with its winning two-hour combination of news, consumer reports, business updates, softer entertainment stories, and book and movie reviews.

Still, theirs was an ego-driven business, and some were not team players. Linus Nazareth certainly fell into that category. He ran *KTA* as his own personal candy store, confident that, as long as he brought in the ratings, his place at KEY was secure. Yelena thought him obnoxious and disrespectful. She disliked his bravado and disapproved of the way he treated his subordinates. Mostly, she kept him on because she didn't want him to go over to the competition. But with a damaged reputation and a loss of credibility, ABC, CBS, and NBC wouldn't want him either.

Yelena pulled her bathrobe from the hook and slid her thick arms into the sleeves.

If she gave Linus enough rope, he would hang himself.

Time wounds all heels.

CHAPTER 30

With the final word still not in regarding the possible contamination of the *KEY to America* studio, the decision had been made to do the Friday morning broadcast from the *Evening Headlines* set. Unit Manager Beth Terry saw to the arrangements.

It had been a slow news cycle, so Linus could go through with his plan to milk the anthrax story, leading with Dr. Lee. Annabelle watched from the control room.

"Yes, Constance, there was a lot of excitement around here yesterday. But all's well that ends well. My aim was to let the public know of the danger that surrounds us, and I think we have done just that."

The host looked at the notes in her lap. "Authorities want to know where you obtained the anthrax. What are you telling them?"

Lee kept the serious expression on his face, though he felt like smiling in smug satisfaction. "I am not going to reveal where I got it. A reporter must protect his sources. If he doesn't, he loses all credibility. Sources have to know they can trust journalists."

Annabelle was nauseated as she listened to the doctor-turned-journalist pontificate, but a glance at the other side of the control room showed that Linus was loving it.

Had Linus felt her eyes upon him? Was that why he looked her way?

"Coming to the party Sunday, Annabelle?" he called over the din of the control room.

It was as if he was trying to put her on the spot, trying to embarrass her. Linus didn't particularly like her, Annabelle knew, and he couldn't care much one way or another if she was a guest in his home. But every staffer was well aware that the annual party at the executive producer's apartment was a command performance. Staffers were afraid not to attend and socialize while watching the football game on the wide-screen TV. Annabelle had heard of the snubs and more-than-coincidental lousy story assignments that followed a missed football party.

"Yes, Linus. I'll be there," she called back and turned her eyes to her clipboard, pretending to be engrossed in her notes.

This was her first party at Linus Nazareth's home. It didn't matter that she'd rather spend a precious Sunday afternoon and evening at home with Mike and the twins. Linus's party was part of the job.

CHAPTER 31

The makeup woman was an annoyance but a necessity, thought Gavin Winston as he peered at his reflection on the mirrored wall. He looked terrible this morning. The bags under his eyes were getting worse, and his skin was blotchy and pasty looking. What did he expect? He hadn't been sleeping well lately.

He'd been hearing the rumblings on the street. And now, this morning, the *Wall Street Journal* article made the rumors a reality. The Securities and Exchange Commission was investigating charges of insider trading at Wellstone, Inc. The investment darling's stock had come tumbling down, causing thousands of small investors to lose millions of dollars. Yet Wellstone executives and their in-the-know friends had sold in the days preceding the fall, not only preserving their initial investments but garnering mammoth profits as well. Once again, the rich got richer, while the little guys were the goats.

As the beige concealer was dabbed beneath his eyes,

Gavin dreaded presenting the Wellstone story in a few minutes. He didn't relish violating a journalistic principle, reporting on a story of which he himself might be considered a part.

The makeup artist removed the nylon cape that protected Gavin's tailored English suit. He bent close to the mirror to adjust the knot on his Ferragamo tie and checked his facial reflection one last time.

He had made a nice piece of change on that Wellstone stock, but it sure wouldn't look good if anyone knew about that.

CHAPTER 32

After the first news block, Constance tossed to Caridad Vega at the weather map.

"Carrie? What will the weekend be like?"

"Well, Constance, winter may actually be a full month away, but those of us in the Northeast are going to be seeing an unusual pre-Thanksgiving snowstorm coming our way." She pointed to the arrows flowing north to south on the map. "There's a cold front coming in from Canada that will be arriving on Saturday night, going into Sunday morning, bringing with it lower-than-normal temperatures for this time of year. So get out your scarves and mittens, folks, and your snow shovels too."

Annabelle wondered, as she listened, if the kids would still fit into last year's boots. She doubted it.

"The rest of the country can expect seasonable temperatures and mostly sunny skies," Carrie finished her report.

Lucky them.

CHAPTER 33

"A dazzling new film.

"Deeply touching.

"Amazing performances.

"People will be talking about *Icicle* for a long time to come."

Coming back to her office to watch the end of the broadcast, Annabelle listened to Russ Parrish toss around the superlatives in his movie review.

Something wasn't right. The movie was supposed to be a

dog. The *New York Times* movie critic had panned *Icicle* in this morning's edition. So had the *Post* and the *Daily News.*

Annabelle clicked the remote, switching her office monitor to another network. At the same time Russ was claiming *Icicle* to be a "must-see," the reviewer at the CBS *Early Show* was calling it "one of the worst films ever."

Sure, reviews were subjective, reactions influenced by the critic's own personal perspective, but how could Russ's view be so dramatically different from all the others?

CHAPTER 34

With thirty more seconds of commercials left to air, Constance read over the copy she would deliver when the camera came back to her, sitting still as the makeup artist repowdered her face. The red light above the camera flashed on, and the stage manager flagged her to begin.

"It's been four decades this weekend since President John F. Kennedy was assassinated as his motorcade drove through Dallas. Many have said that it was the day that our country lost its innocence."

The video package began to roll with a narration Constance had recorded earlier playing over the archive material. The young, handsome president and his stylish young wife getting off the plane, the roses presented to Jackie, the beaming couple sitting in the back of the open limousine. Then the grainy black-and-white film of the school book depository, the speeding police cars, the Texans crying on the grassy knoll, the flowers lying forgotten on the bloodied backseat of the presidential car.

I wasn't even born yet, thought Annabelle as she watched the monitor and waited for Constance to come back on camera.

"But for a younger generation of Americans, September eleventh is the day that they will remember as the beginning of *their* loss of innocence. And many still suffer from depression, anxiety, and, for some, post-traumatic stress disorder as a result of the horror of that day."

Mike is in that number, as if I needed any reminder, Annabelle noted dully. She had read that almost half a million New Yorkers had suffered from depression directly attributable to September 11. Nearly three thousand people had been killed in one fell swoop. All of those people had mothers and fathers, many had wives and husbands and sons and daughters and aunts and uncles and cousins who were now called on to live with the loss and the savage memories and somehow keep going.

Three hundred forty-three New York firefighters, one out of every thirty-three, all dead. Three hundred forty-three brothers and sisters who had made the supreme sacrifice. The ones who had survived said it was with them constantly, they never forgot about it, missing their buddies. Survivors' guilt plagued the lucky ones. Why them, why not me?

Once happy to go to work, secure in the camaraderie of the firehouse, these well-trained men had taken satisfaction from performing an important job. Now, they were haunted by the thoughts of their departed friends and lost sleep at night wondering what could have been done differently. If the command structure had been more unified, if the radios had worked, if the buildings hadn't collapsed. If, if, if.

Twenty percent of Americans knew someone hurt or killed in the attacks, and the ripples were still being felt in the society at large. Many had lost their jobs owing to the attacks, never to reclaim them. Applications to the CIA and the Peace Corps were up dramatically. So were the hate crimes reported to the Council on American-Islamic Relations.

Annabelle knew all this because she couldn't stop reading about it. If Mike had shut down, she kept thinking, it was important for her to immerse herself. The more she understood, the more she might be able to help him. But each time she brought up anything related to September 11, urging him to talk about it and let it out, Mike would either yell or, worse as far as she was concerned, clam up tight.

Watching the sanitized file tape roll, edited to omit the most gruesome scenes of people actually jumping out the windows to avoid burning to death, Annabelle could only imagine what her husband had witnessed that day. Only imagine it, because Mike refused to share the unspeakable horrors that tormented him.

CHAPTER 35

When the show ended, Annabelle went down to the cafeteria and filled two take-out cups with Starbucks coffee. The milk dispenser was already empty.

"Edgar, I hate to trouble you, but I need some milk."

"No trouble at all, miss."

He offered her a fresh container of milk and waited while she poured the white liquid into the coffees.

"Thank you very much," she said, handing the carton back. "I appreciate it."

He smiled at her as he began to empty the rest of the milk into the dispenser. That was one nice lady. Not like the others, who didn't even give him the time of day.

At the salad bar, Annabelle was filling a plastic bowl with

sliced fruit when a woman and two young boys dressed in ski jackets pushed through the cafeteria turnstile.

"Uncle Edgar!" exclaimed the slightly smaller one, running to the food-service worker and throwing his arms around the grown man's waist.

"How's my Willie?" asked Edgar, grinning and hugging the child. "Happy birthday, my boy."

The older boy held back but smiled as he stood next to his mother. Annabelle estimated the brothers to be three and four years old. It was rare to see little ones inside the Broadcast Center. When children did venture in, they were treated as curiosities, mesmerizing to watch.

"Take a look over there, boys, and see what you'd like to eat," instructed Edgar, nodding toward the salad bar. "I'll go toast some bagels for you."

As Edgar went to the grill, the mother and her children began to fill their tray.

"I want the pineapple," said the older boy.

"I want the bananas," declared Willie. "And grape jelly for my bagel."

The mother, feeling Annabelle watching, looked up and smiled tentatively. Annabelle returned the smile. "It's a big treat to come in to visit their uncle, isn't it?" she asked. "I know my kids are so excited if I bring them into the office."

The last time Annabelle had brought Thomas and Tara in, Constance had arranged for them to sit on the set with her after the broadcast while the cameras recorded them.

The twins still got a big charge out of playing back the videotape of themselves on television. Annabelle wished she could have offered to do the same for Edgar's nephews, but with the upset at *KTA* right now, that wasn't a possibility.

Instead, she turned to the younger boy and said, "Happy birthday, Willie. I hope you have fun today."

Annabelle was waiting when Constance, stunning now in full makeup, arrived back at her office.

"Oooh. Just what I needed," said Constance, accepting the paper cup of piping hot high-test. She popped off the plastic lid and settled back in her chair. "So how's it going, honey?" she asked, taking a careful sip.

Annabelle rolled her eyes. "I can't tell. I think the FBI believed me when I told them I had nothing to do with Lee's plan. I only hope Yelena did. I need this job, Constance."

The show host nodded. "How *is* it going at home?"

"I'm still waiting for Mike's new medication to kick in. It's been over two weeks now. Of course, he'd actually have to take the medicine in order for it to work." She sighed heavily.

"I don't know what to say, Annabelle. It sounds lame, but I know everything will work out. Mike is such a great guy. He will pull out of this. I'm sure of it."

"I hope you're right, because the whole thing is really getting to me." She felt tears welling.

"I don't know how you handle it all, Annabelle. I admire you so."

Annabelle managed a laugh. "You've got to be kidding. You? Admire *me*? You're the one with the stellar career and the face and personality the country loves."

"Yeah, yeah, that's all well and good and, believe me, I know how lucky I am to be in this position. But I can concentrate on my work with no distractions. I have no one else depending on me like you do."

"Is that a good thing or a bad thing?"

Constance considered the question. "Neither, I guess. It's just the way it is. Who knows how I'd feel if I had met my Prince Charming, a man that I loved so much I wanted to get married and raise a couple of kids. But I haven't so far, and that's okay with me. I like where I'm at. Which reminds me..." She opened a pharmacy bottle and swallowed a pill.

"What's that?"

"Cipro. I decided to take it. I'm not taking any chances."

Annabelle held back from making a judgment. Who knew how she would feel if a tube of anthrax had been thrust in her face?

They finished their coffees, talking about what an idiot John Lee was and speculating on whether, in the end, this episode would be good for his career.

"I've got to go meet with him now." Annabelle moaned, rising from the sofa.

"Good luck, baby." Constance picked up the telephone. "I've got a few calls to make, and then I'm cutting out of here early. I'm flying down to D.C. to see my mother."

Annabelle stopped at the door. "Please. Don't tell me you're not going to Linus's party."

"I wish. I don't really want to go, but I have to attend. Linus would have a fit if I didn't. I'll take the shuttle back Sunday afternoon in time to be there."

"Good. Because I need the moral support," Annabelle declared.

Constance gave a wry smile and shook her head. "I could use some support too, my friend. How much fun do you think it is to know that I will have to watch Lauren Adams batting her baby blues at Linus? I know full well that she's salivating for my job and thinks that's the way to get it."

"No way, Constance, will Lauren ever get your spot." Annabelle was adamant. "She doesn't hold a candle to you and we both know it."

"Never say never, Annabelle. We both know, in this business, stranger things have happened."

CHAPTER 36

"You're kidding, right?"

Joe Connelly had a hard time believing what he was hearing through the telephone receiver. It was incredible but, according to the health department, true. He hung up the phone and digested the information.

He popped an antacid tablet into his mouth, not relishing the task before him. He didn't want to tell Yelena. She would be livid, and she would have every right to be. How could KEY News be taken seriously after something like this? The media critics would have a field day, not to mention the erosion of the viewers' trust.

And how stupid could Dr. Lee possibly be? Hadn't he known that the truth would come out?

The lab tests showed that the white powder in the vial Lee proclaimed to be anthrax was nothing more than run-of-the-mill confectioners' sugar.

CHAPTER

37

Annabelle was sitting next to John Lee when Yelena Gregory herself tracked them down in a screening room. The arrogance drained from Lee's face as he listened to the news.

"That's impossible. There must be some mistake, Yelena," he sputtered.

"I'll say, John. That's the understatement of the millennium. There was one big, devastating, helluva mistake." The president's voice was low and even, but Annabelle noticed that Yelena's hand was trembling.

"Unless my source completely screwed me..." Lee was frantic.

"Well, there definitely was some screwing done here, John, and KEY News was the recipient. A respected news organization that has spent decades building its reputation and gaining the public trust now has to report that our correspondent perpetrated a miserable, despicable hoax."

Lee's face was ashen. "I swear, Yelena. I had no idea that

there was sugar in that container. I thought it was the real deal. You have to believe that," he pleaded.

"I don't have to believe anything. You're out, effective immediately."

CHAPTER 38

There were lots of picture frames on *KTA* Unit Manager Beth Terry's desk, but none of the children who beamed from them were truly her own. Nieces, nephews, and godchildren delighted in their "Auntie Beth," who never forgot a birthday, holiday, or other special occasion, always sending the best gifts. Not the practical things like pajamas or slippers, but the fun things like the latest toys and video games. When Auntie Beth came bearing her gifts, the kids always knew they were going to be good.

Beth took pride in her shopping prowess, stalking not just F.A.O. Schwarz but most of the other Fifth Avenue stores as well. Bergdorf's, Bendel's, Lord & Taylor, and Saks were her weekend haunts. She knew by heart which merchandise was on which floor and when the best sales were scheduled to run. When *KTA* staffers needed gift ideas or guidance on where to find the garment they were searching for, they came to Beth.

She was well into her Christmas shopping. And why shouldn't she be, she asked herself as she stirred her nonfat vanilla yogurt before the morning meeting and perused her mostly checked-off list. The shopping provided a sense of purpose, a weekend diversion. It wasn't as if her dance card was full on Saturdays and Sundays. The people with children had soccer games, scouting trips, and school fairs to attend. The ones without kids but with significant others in their lives had Saturday night dates and long, leisurely Sunday brunches to savor. While Manhattan provided fabulous museums and the best theater in the world, it seemed everything was enjoyed best when shared.

And while many people dreaded Monday mornings, Beth was relieved when the workweek started. She felt most alive, most happy when she was doing her job, coordinating logistics, satellite bookings, and travel arrangements, solving budget problems and the myriad other details that had to be attended to in order to get *KTA* on the air each morning. And, perhaps more to the point, Mondays meant she would be with Linus again.

She clung to the hope that it would eventually work out between them though, if she were really honest with herself, she had to admit that Linus had never alluded to marriage. But every time her boss said, "I don't know what I'd do without you, Beth," or "I'm so lucky to have you, Beth," or put his hand on her shoulder when they went over broadcast plans, she dreamed. Others might have been frightened of him, criticized him, or despised him, but for Beth, Linus Nazareth was all she could possibly want in a man. She knew a side of him that others did not know.

She was only too happy to be doing his Christmas shopping for him again this year. But even with the time she had to fill, she was going to have to do some shopping on the Web to get it all done. Beth clicked on the computer's Internet browser and "let her fingers do the walking."

CHAPTER 39

Every so often, Yelena made it a point to sit in on a *KTA* morning meeting. Today, she wanted to hear what Linus was going to say to the staff about the anthrax hoax. She took a seat at the table along with the news employees and waited.

Linus came into the conference room, ruddy-faced and palming his football. His tie was loosened, and his shirtsleeves were rolled up. He was ready for business.

Tossing the football at Russ, who fumbled it, Linus let out an angry oath.

"That's the story of this show lately. Incomplete passes. And that's going to stop now."

There was silence in the room while the *KTA* staff waited.

"We have been made laughingstocks by John Lee's shenanigans. As you all have undoubtedly heard by now, his anthrax was only sugar, his investigative journalism a fraud. We are all tainted by this, and we have to make up for it. I will not be the coach of a losing team."

No one said a word.

Linus picked up the football that Russ had placed on the table, tossed it in the air, and caught it.

"Our viewers have to trust us. They can't be turning their dials to another network for their news in the morning. *KEY to America* has become a leader in our time slot, and I intend it to stay that way. We cannot skip a beat now. We have to try harder than ever. Next week people will be tuning in to see how we are going to handle ourselves, and I promise you this: We are going to give them one helluva week of television. We are going to educate and entertain and rivet them. They are going to be so satisfied that they won't need to look anywhere else and will forget about our mistake."

He nodded at the anchorwoman. "Constance, I know I can count on you to be your most charming, energetic, engaging self. And, Harry, just keep on doing what you do so well," he said, stroking his other cohost's ego. "As for the rest of you, I expect each and every one of you to give one hundred and ten percent. I will accept nothing less. Anyone who doesn't come up with the goods can look for another job."

Around the table, eyes were averted.

"All right now. Dominick, why don't you outline the plans for next week?"

The senior producer, Linus's second in command, explained the theme for Thanksgiving week: "Holidays in the Big Apple." Each morning, Constance and Harry would be on location at a Manhattan landmark. Monday, Radio City; Tuesday, the Statue of Liberty and Ellis Island; Wednesday, the clever and opulent Christmas window displays at the city's department stores; Thursday, the legendary Macy's Thanksgiving Day Parade. Friday's venue was still undecided.

"It's traditionally the biggest shopping day of the year," offered Dominick. "We can do something from Fifth Avenue if we want."

"Or just come back to the studio," Gavin interjected. "Are people even watching television on the morning after Thanksgiving?"

Linus spiked the football into the carpet. "I don't give a damn if they are or they aren't," he shouted. "We do this show as if they have nothing at all better in the world to do. That's the last day of sweeps. We don't slack off. Remember," Linus quoted the old football proverb for the umpteenth time as the news staffers groaned silently. "Winning isn't everything. It's the *only* thing."

For the remainder of the meeting, no one dared utter anything other than the most positive, can-do suggestions. A half hour later, the meeting concluded, Annabelle and the others were gathering their belongings to leave.

"Hold on, Annabelle." Linus's gruff tone startled her, and she knocked over her tote bag, the contents spilling across the conference table. Flustered, she reclaimed Jerome's rubber-banded manuscript and slid it hastily back into her bag as her coworkers streamed past.

The executive producer tossed the pigskin into the air one last time. "Since you don't have a correspondent to work with right now, Annabelle, I want you to field-produce on the location shoots next week. Talk to Dominick. He'll tell you what to do."

CHAPTER 40

Midway through the executive producer's rantings, Gavin stopped listening and started fantasizing. He stared at the intern who sat quietly in the corner of the conference room, listening wide-eyed as Linus vented.

Lily was far too sweet for this business, he thought, wanting to caress her soft, shining blond hair. She should marry well and bear beautiful children who looked just like her. She should be treasured and taken care of by a man who appreciated her endearing qualities. She should live happily ever after in a comfortable home behind a white picket fence with a station wagon in the garage and a big dog sleeping peacefully in front of the fireplace.

Gavin daydreamed about what it would be like to be the man who came home to golden Lily each night. How wonderful that would be, how perfect. But, alas, he feared that Lily was the same as all the others he had pursued during their internships at *KTA*. These young girls attended good colleges and thought they wanted big careers in the glamorous world of television news. Lily had told him as much last night when he had finally talked her into going out for that drink with him.

Lily had it all planned. After graduation, she would start out as a reporter in a small station and work her way up through the larger local markets until she arrived, in a very few years, at the network level. Barbara Walters, Diane Sawyer, Constance Young, Eliza Blake, beware. Lily is gunning for your jobs.

Gavin had pretended to take her seriously, not letting on that he thought her prattle naïve and tiresome. *I'm not interested in your mind or your career,* he'd ached to shout. Instead, he nodded gravely and volunteered to help her any way he could.

Once the endless meeting was over, Gavin went to his office, booted up his computer, and began to type.

DEAR LILY:
I REALLY ENJOYED THE TIME WE SPENT TOGETHER LAST EVENING. IT WAS A PLEASURE GETTING TO KNOW YOU BETTER. YOU ARE AN AMAZING YOUNG WOMAN AND I SUSPECT YOU HAVE BIG THINGS IN FRONT OF YOU.
YOU HAVE CHOSEN TO MAKE YOUR WAY IN A VERY TOUGH, COMPETITIVE BUSINESS, LILY, A BUSINESS WHERE IT IS HELPFUL TO HAVE SOMEONE WHO TAKES AN INTEREST IN YOU AND WORKS TO BRING YOU ALONG. I COULD BE THAT PERSON FOR YOU, LILY. I WOULD LIKE TO BE THAT PERSON. BUT, IN ORDER FOR ME TO GUIDE YOU, IT WILL BE NECESSARY FOR ME TO BECOME MORE FAMILIAR WITH YOUR STRENGTHS AND TO IDENTIFY YOUR WEAKNESSES. IT WOULD BE A GOOD THING IF WE SPENT MORE TIME TOGETHER.
LET'S PLAN TO HAVE DINNER NEXT WEEK. HOW ABOUT MONDAY NIGHT?
BEST,
GAVIN

He typed in the e-mail address Lily had been assigned for the duration of her internship at KEY and sent his suggestion on its way.

CHAPTER 41

Two uniformed security guards stood at the doorway of John Lee's newly reopened office, waiting to escort him from the building while Annabelle helped him fill the cardboard boxes that had been provided for packing his personal possessions.

This was so humiliating. Annabelle winced as she took Lee's medical school diploma from the wall. One day you're waltzing through the lobby, flashing your ID to enter the heady world of broadcast journalism, the next you're persona non grata, the enemy, forbidden inside. She had heard stories of others who had been hurried out the door like this, given the literal bum's rush, but she had never actually seen it happen. She hoped she never would again. Annabelle couldn't stand John Lee, but she wouldn't wish this on anyone.

"I can't carry all this stuff with me, Annabelle."

"I know. I'll have the attendants come, and we'll send the cartons of books and things to your apartment. In fact, if you want to get out of here, I'll finish packing up."

"Okay, but I want to clean out my desk myself."

As he cleared the Rolodex and clock from the desktop, the phone rang. Annabelle pretended to be preoccupied with taking books from the shelves as she overheard Lee's angry half of the conversation.

"It's about time you returned my call." The doctor's voice cracked. "How the hell could you do this to me, telling me it was anthrax when it wasn't?

"Don't give me that crap. There was no anthrax in there. It was powdered sugar.

"No, it's not impossible. The lab tests were conclusive.

"Well, if you swear that what you gave me was anthrax, then where the hell is it?"

CHAPTER 42

The risk had been enormous, but there was no way that the swap could have been done at home; the chance of contamination there was unacceptable. If the authorities found traces of anthrax in the Broadcast Center, they would attribute them to Dr. Lee's stunt and clean up the mess.

Yes, it had been a good call to do it all right here in the building. It had worked out so effortlessly, really, costing next to nothing. The bonanza of finding the anthrax so easily in the drawer in John Lee's office, the scanning of the Internet for a crash course in handling the deadly white powder, the trip to the biohazard supply store for the masks and the gloves. Even the children's chemistry set sent by the toy manufacturer as a sample for promotion had shown up at precisely the right time, its small glass test tubes indistinguishable from the one in Lee's desk.

The Broadcast Center was a sprawling building with subterranean layers of storage rooms and forgotten closets. One of those served as the convenient, hidden workshop.

There had been only one hitch, one thing that should have been done differently. It would have been better to pick up the confectioners' sugar at the supermarket instead of sneaking into the cafeteria and filching it there. That mistake had the potential of ruining everything.

And there was another loose end that needed to be tidied up as well. That manuscript couldn't stay in Annabelle's bag forever. After Jerome died, Annabelle could bring his vile diatribe to a publisher herself, or she could go ahead and write her own book.

CHAPTER 43

The press information department issued Yelena Gregory's statement, and a half hour later Annabelle read on her computer screen the text from the Associated Press.

> TESTS CONDUCTED BY THE NEW YORK CITY HEALTH DEPARTMENT ON THE SUBSTANCE CLAIMED TO BE ANTHRAX BY DR. JOHN LEE ON THE KEY NEWS BROADCAST *KEY TO AMERICA* REVEAL THAT THE TEST TUBE ACTUALLY CONTAINED POWDERED SUGAR. KEY NEWS DISAVOWS THE HOAX PERPETRATED BY DR. LEE AND HAS TERMINATED HIS ASSOCIATION WITH, AND EMPLOYMENT BY, KEY NEWS.

Short, and not so sweet.

Now she knew where this was going to leave her, at least for the time being. Since she had no medical correspondent to work with, Linus expected her to field-produce. Familiarizing herself with the locations they were shooting and suggesting angles for their coverage wouldn't be a problem.

Annabelle knew her city well, but it sure wouldn't be fun standing out in the freezing cold New York Harbor on Tuesday morning.

She glanced at her watch, eager for one o'clock to come. She hadn't had lunch with Constance in quite a while, and she wanted to catch up on everything that had been happening. They were only going up the street to the little Greek restaurant, but at least it was an opportunity to talk without interruption, away from the KEY News crowd.

As she was putting on her coat, the phone rang and she stopped to answer it. "Annabelle Murphy speaking."

"This is Essex Hills Hospital. We have you listed as the emergency contact for a Jerome Henning."

"Yes?" she answered with trepidation. It couldn't be good if they were calling the emergency contact. Her mind raced. Jerome's parents had died while she was dating him. He had only one sibling, a brother who lived on the West Coast. She was touched that Jerome had put her down to be the person to call in an emergency.

"Hold on one moment, please. The doctor would like to speak with you."

Oh my God—Jerome. Annabelle felt her face grow hot. What kind of friend was she, so consumed by what was happening in her immediate world that she hadn't tried again to check on Jerome? She hadn't been overly concerned. After all, it was just a virus or the flu, wasn't it? There was so much of all that going around this season.

The doctor was on the line now, and she listened in disbelief.

"Mr. Henning is in critical condition. He's on a ventilator to help him breathe but, quite honestly, the prognosis is not good."

Annabelle tried to stay calm. "What's wrong with him?"

"We've just notified the health department, and as the one he's listed to be informed of his condition, you have a right to know as well. The blood culture indicates anthrax exposure."

CHAPTER 44

"Fiona Simon on line three" came the call from the intercom.

Linus punched the lit extension button. "Fiona," he called. "How's it going?"

"I'm fine, Linus. The question is, how are you?"

"Oh, you mean the anthrax thing?" He made a concerted effort to sound nonchalant. "Not to worry. It will blow over."

"People are talking about it, Linus. I was thinking we might include something about it in your book."

Linus was alarmed. There was no way he wanted this fiasco immortalized.

"Isn't it too late for that, Fiona?" He searched for a way out. "The editing is all done."

"True, and I have the advance reading copies all set to send over to you. But we could add another chapter on this anthrax thing before we go to press with the hard covers."

He had to buy himself some time to figure a way out. He didn't like refusing Fiona again. He'd already said no when she had pleaded with him to include the heartbreaking story of Seth's accident, an account sure to hook readers.

"Let me think about it, Fiona, all right? In the meantime, when can I see the reading copies?"

"I'll messenger them over. To your office?"

"No. Send them to my home." He rattled off the Central Park West address.

Good. He'd have them to give out at the party on Sunday.

Linus barked out to his secretary. "Get Russ Parrish on the line, will you? And tell him I want to see him right away."

It took less than two minutes for the entertainment correspondent to arrive.

"Close the door," Linus commanded, "and take a seat."

Russ obeyed.

"First of all, you're lucky that I didn't rip into you in front of everyone at the meeting this morning."

Russ looked at his boss with trepidation. "Rip into me about what?" he managed to ask.

"About that ridiculous review of yours this morning."

"I don't know what you're talking about, Linus."

"Oh, you don't? What was it again? 'A dazzling new film'? 'Amazing performances'? That's a crock and we both know it, Russ. I got a copy of the movie too. *Icicle* is a piece of crap."

"That's your opinion, Linus," Russ defended himself. "I thought otherwise."

"Well, you may have 'thought otherwise,'" Linus imitated with sarcasm, "though I would hope you have better taste than that. But the bottom line is, our viewers listen to your reviews to decide what they are going to spend their entertainment money on. If you steer them wrong, they aren't going to listen to you anymore, and that's bad for the show. And what's bad for the show has to go."

Russ waited, desperately wanting to escape to his office and the comfort of his soft white powder.

"So, I'm telling you like it is, Russ," Linus continued. "Another one of those bogus reviews and you're history."

CHAPTER 45

In light of everything else that was going on at KEY News, Yelena knew some would sneer at the e-mail she was about to send out. But she wanted to get on record on this subject. It concerned her that so many employees were conducting personal business on company time.

FROM: YELENA GREGORY
TO: ALL PERSONNEL

USE OF KEY NEWS COMPUTER FACILITIES IS PERMITTED FOR LEGITIMATE AND APPROPRIATE PURPOSES ONLY. THESE INCLUDE: JOURNALISTIC RESEARCH, COMPANY-RELATED ACTIVITIES, AND OTHER USES APPROPRIATE FOR A NEWS ORGANIZATION. *NOT* INCLUDED IS USE OF COMPUTER FACILITIES FOR PERSONAL SHOPPING. AS THE HOLIDAY SEASON APPROACHES, ALL KEY NEWS PERSONNEL ARE REMINDED THAT YOUR COMPUTER IS NOT TO BE USED FOR HOLIDAY SHOPPING PURPOSES.

Yelena read the message over again and hit the Send button.

CHAPTER 46

Before she left to go to the hospital, Annabelle stopped at the news president's office, anticipating she would be breaking the news about Jerome to Yelena. But Yelena had already heard. Joe Connelly sat with her. The health department in New Jersey had informed its New York City counterpart, which had, in turn, alerted KEY's security department.

"That's it. All of the *KEY to America* offices are to be evacuated for testing, and I want every single one of the staff tested for anthrax exposure," Yelena commanded. "I don't care if it's warranted or not. We are not taking any chances."

The security chief nodded. "We can set up the station for nasal swabs to be taken in the cafeteria."

"Fine." Yelena sighed. "At least we can be grateful that it's Friday. *KTA* doesn't have to be on the air again until Monday morning. Hopefully we will have an all-clear by then."

CHAPTER

47

"Don't you dare come home, Gavin. I mean it. I don't want you bringing home anything with you," his wife screeched through the phone.

"Even if I have been exposed, Marguerite, it's not contagious. I won't pass it on to you."

"It might be on your clothes or something."

"Leave some clothes out in the garage. I'll change before I come inside."

"Absolutely not, Gavin." She was adamant. "I would think that you'd want to protect me."

There was no use fighting or rationalizing with her. Marguerite's mind was made up. Gavin had learned over the course of their interminable marriage that it was easier to let Marguerite have her own way. He might be the man from whom American viewers got their morning financial news, the man who had marshaled the Winstons' money into hefty bank accounts, but in his own home Marguerite called the shots. Otherwise, his life was misery.

It wasn't even that Marguerite was trying to protect their children. They had no kids to worry about. Just that damned dog, Gigi. Marguerite doted on the poodle, but that miserable little thing reminded Gavin more of a rat than a dog. He wouldn't shed a tear if Gigi snorted a little anthrax.

Gavin snapped off his cell phone and got in line at the cafeteria annex to wait his turn for his nasal swab.

No wonder he had to look for affection wherever he could find it.

CHAPTER 48

The soft, rhythmic sound of the ventilator pulsed through the hospital room. Annabelle was allowed only a few minutes to stand beside Jerome's bed.

He wasn't going to get better.

She watched him lying there, so still now beneath the thin cotton blanket. Thought of him just the day before, so eager to hear what she thought about his treasured manuscript. He'd spent so much time on it. Therapy, he'd said. Something to concentrate on and vent his frustrations with the lunacy at work, something to look forward to getting published, something to take his mind off the years of yearning for Annabelle.

She'd cut him off, changing the subject, when he told her that. She was married to Mike, loved Mike and their children more than she had ever thought possible. Though, admittedly, they were going through a rough patch right now, she was committed to her family. She knew that. But there had been times, in the middle of the night, when Mike, unable to sleep, prowled the apartment and Annabelle lay by herself, wondering what her life would have been like if she had chosen Jerome instead.

Always, the first thing that came to mind was that she wouldn't have Thomas and Tara. Because of that, no matter how things worked out with Mike, Annabelle was certain that she had no regrets.

She reached down and gently pushed the brown hair back from Jerome's smooth forehead. So young, so smart, so strong, and yet so ill-equipped to fight his way back from this.

Jerome had thought he was invincible. Willing to take chances, determined to live large. From that first day she had met him at the videotape library, early in their careers at KEY, Annabelle had been attracted to his almost boundless energy, inquisitive dark eyes, and easy smile.

Jerome was a party boy. That was his strength and his weakness. With his sense of adventure, his curiosity and enthusiasm about trying new things and visiting new places, he was fun to be around. Together they were always sampling the latest ethnic restaurants or planning interesting excursions for their days off work.

But catching Jerome using drugs had turned Annabelle off. She wasn't a prude and enjoyed a drink herself once in a while, but cocaine scared her. No good could come of it. Jerome had assured her he would stop and, eventually, he had. But not before Annabelle had broken off their relationship. And then she had met Mike.

Again, work had proved to be the matchmaker for Annabelle. She had been sent downtown to do a story on fire safety. Mike had been one of several firefighters she'd interviewed, but he was the only one she'd felt the immediate pull toward as he good-naturedly demonstrated the fire equipment for the camera. He was so earnest in his explanations, so seemingly sure that his was one of the most important jobs in the world. His passion for helping people came through loud and clear, and Annabelle found herself hooked.

She gave him her business card on the pretext he could phone her if he thought of anything else she should include in her piece. The next day Mike did call, not to add to the news story but to ask her out for dinner. From then on, they had been almost inseparable.

Jerome had taken it hard.

How had everything gotten so complicated, so messed

up? The most important man in her life was trapped in the dark hell of depression, while another she still cared about was losing the fight for his life.

Annabelle struggled to make sense of what was happening, her mind trying to recall the facts about inhalation anthrax. Jerome had been sick earlier in the week, then felt better for a day, then had a recurrence. Classic symptoms. But the incubation period between exposure and symptoms was at least two days. That would mean the latest he could have been exposed to the anthrax spores was the end of last week, not yesterday, when there was all the excitement about Dr. Lee's anthrax display. A display that turned out to have been a fake.

If Lee had been telling the truth and his confederate at the lab had really given him the deadly powder, what had happened to it? Where was the anthrax now? And how had Jerome been exposed?

And, if Jerome had been exposed, who else might be?

CHAPTER

49

She had wanted to go directly home from the hospital but then realized she couldn't. She had to go back to the Broadcast Center and get that mandatory nasal swab taken. Annabelle toyed with the idea of ignoring Yelena's order. But if they were keeping a list of who was tested, as they undoubtedly would be, Annabelle didn't like the prospect of being called on the carpet for noncompliance. Plus, it didn't really hurt to get checked.

It was already dark as she released the car service at the curb in front of the building. A biting wind blew from the Hudson River, up the wide corridor of Fifty-seventh Street. Annabelle pushed through the revolving door into the lobby, glad to be in warmth again, slid her identification card across the electronic scanner, and waited for the beeping signal. She took the stairs from the lobby down to the long hallway that led to the cafeteria.

There was no wait. Everybody must have made it a point

to get down for their tests while on company time, wanting to get out as early as they could on a Friday night.

"Am I the last one?" Annabelle asked the nurse.

The medical professional consulted the printed list on the desk. "No, there are still a few others who haven't come in yet."

Annabelle stood dutifully as the stick was inserted in her nose. She hoped this would turn out to be a complete waste of her time.

Back on the sidewalk outside the Broadcast Center, Annabelle pulled on the gloves she took from her tote bag and wondered if she should hail a taxi. It would be nice to take a cab, but the traffic going downtown on a Friday night was sure to be heavy. The meter would just tick away. Conscious of their family's tight budget, Annabelle headed for the subway.

Fifty-seventh Street was still congested with cars heading for the on-ramp to the backed-up West Side Highway. The other direction was not much better, with motorists heading to Broadway or farther east to the twinkling holiday lights of Fifth Avenue. As she moved along the wide sidewalk, Annabelle's long strides almost kept pace with the snail-like progress of the vehicles. She passed restaurants, clothing stores, and apartment buildings. People entered and exited, all had lives and problems of their own. By the end of the second long block, her mind on Jerome, Annabelle didn't feel the cold.

She slipped her subway pass from the zippered compartment of her wallet and stuck it in the turnstile. Debris littered the jammed platform and floated in the gust of air that swooshed through the tunnel as the train pulled into the station. A crush of riders pushed forward as the car doors opened. *Let 'em off first,* she thought. As she moved to board the train, Annabelle felt herself being shoved forward, and her tote bag was yanked out of her hand.

She turned in the direction of the force, searching the faces in the rush-hour crowd, catching sight of a dark coat with a hood pulled up heading toward the steps as the subway doors closed, trapping Annabelle helplessly inside.

CHAPTER 50

With Christmas coming and budget cutbacks making overtime scarce, Edgar could use all the extra hours he could get. His sister had two young kids and a husband who was on the lam, leaving Edgar as the male figure in his nephews' lives. He relished playing Santa Claus, determined that the boys would have as good a holiday as possible despite the fact that their father was a miserable lowlife. But that dream cost money, and when someone from the night shift called in sick, Edgar dutifully volunteered to do a double.

The cafeteria was normally fairly quiet during the evenings, night-shift staffers preferring to order take-out dinners from the pizza joints and Chinese restaurants in the area. Tonight, there was more activity than usual as the last *KTA* staffers straggled through on their way to get their noses swabbed. Edgar got in line himself. He'd spent a lot of time on the *KTA* floor and, after all, the tests were free. Why take any chances?

By nine o'clock the health workers had packed up their testing paraphernalia and gone. The grill was turned off at ten and the cook went home, leaving Edgar to empty the coffee urns, wipe the counters, and lock everything up for the night.

As he went to switch off the lights in the kitchen, he noticed an industrial-size pot soaking in the large sink. He didn't want the guy who opened up in the morning to be greeted by that. Edgar rolled up his sleeves.

A turn of the faucet sent the hot water rushing into the stainless-steel sink. The noise of the pounding liquid and of the pot hitting the sink's sides as Edgar scrubbed blocked out any warning sounds.

He was rinsing away the soap when he felt the piercing pain between his shoulder blades.

CHAPTER 51

After Annabelle had tucked the kids into their beds for the night and cleaned up the kitchen, she looked forward to a good long soak in the bathtub. She wished she had some exotic, luxurious concoction to pour beneath the spigot, but Mr. Bubble and Epsom salts would have to do.

As she slipped off her bathrobe, Annabelle winced. Her shoulder was aching. The tote bag had been pulled away from her with great force, yanking her arm along with it. Thank goodness, at least whoever it was hadn't gotten her purse as well. Alerting all the credit card companies and getting a new driver's license was a headache she was glad to avoid.

The thief was probably cursing his choice of target. Perhaps the bag had already been tossed in a trash can. There were only papers in it, nothing of any apparent value to someone else, only things that mattered to Annabelle and Jerome. Annabelle closed her eyes and sank down beneath the hot water as she thought of Jerome's precious manuscript lying exposed in a garbage can on some dark city street.

Well, she wouldn't have to explain the theft to him now.

There was a soft tapping at the bathroom door.

"Come in," she called, fully expecting to see Thomas or Tara up for a glass of water or to tell her that a bad dream had woken them. Instead, the door opened and Mike stood before her. She looked at him inquisitively.

"Just checking to see if you're all right."

"A little sore, but otherwise I'm fine."

He lowered his tall frame to sit on the edge of the tub.

"I don't know what we'd do, what I'd do, if anything happened to you, Annabelle." His eyes welled up as he reached down and brushed her face with the back of his hand.

This was the first sign of affection he had shown her in such a long time. He'd been so enmeshed in his dark thoughts, incapable of focusing on what was going on outside his tortured inner world. What she and the children needed was beyond his concentration. They had been living in parallel worlds: Annabelle's rooted in the reality of young children's schedules, keeping a house, going to work, paying the bills; Mike's twisted with the memories of carnage and death and helplessness.

"Nothing is going to happen to me, sweetheart. I'm right here, and you can't get rid of me." She brought his hand to her lips.

Maybe this was a good sign. Maybe he was starting to come around. Maybe, please God, the old Mike was coming back to her. She missed him so.

"Some guys from the firehouse came over today," he offered.

Annabelle's face brightened. "Really? Great."

Mike frowned. "No, it's not so great. There's talk that the mayor wants to close our firehouse to balance the budget. They want me to help them fight it."

"What did you say?" Annabelle held her breath, waiting for his answer.

"I told them I'd think about it."

At least he didn't outright refuse. Another good sign. Maybe that medicine was beginning to work.

CHAPTER 52

It was after midnight as Linus poured himself another glass of vodka. He wasn't the least bit tired. There was no use going to bed, where he would only toss and turn.

Walking into the library, he played with the idea of giving Lauren a call but thought better of it. Her boyfriend was coming in from Chicago this weekend. Lauren and Linus had an unspoken rule. During the week they could flirt their little brains out, but when the investment banker beau came to town, Linus was not to interrupt. Besides, he would look lonely and pathetic if he called this late.

Lauren was a shrewd one. She had sized up the situation with Linus from the start. He was married to his work, and everything else was merely a distraction. His widower's status made him the treasured extra man at dinner parties, but matchmakers had tried repeatedly and unsuccessfully to make him part of a long-lasting couple. He enjoyed the cat-and-mouse games of flirting and dating, but another marriage was the last thing on his mind.

Why would he ever want to marry again, he wondered, as he popped a cassette into the video deck and settled back on the bloodred leather sofa. He had gotten everything he wanted the first time around. Suzanne had been attractive, energetic, and smart, although too sensitive. Her family had vaults of money; her father was heavily invested in Manhattan real estate. Here he still sat in the gift Suzanne's dad had given them, to get them out of the suburbs afterward, to make them forget. A three-floor apartment in the Majestic, facing out over Central Park. The old man had been generous when he died as well, leaving them enough money to take care of his beloved grandson for the rest of his life, at home, not in some impersonal, uncontrollable institution.

The beginning years had been good ones. The twins were born just a year after they were married. Suzanne was content with double motherhood and playing Susie Homemaker in the suburbs while Linus worked on his television career. That he was constantly on call and traveling all the time didn't seem to bother her. The kids were her world.

And when the world came crashing down, Suzanne never really got over it, he thought, as he leaned down to stroke the thick fur of the Irish setter who sat at his feet. She went through the motions, continuing to raise Wayne and tend to Seth, getting involved in the parental activities at school, trying to make birthdays and holidays festive occasions. But Linus couldn't remember ever seeing her laugh again. Smiles, yes, but full, hearty laughter, never.

It was as if she had held on just as long as she could. After Wayne went off to college that first time, Suzanne had given up. The quiet apartment left her too much time to think. She'd stare out the picture windows, not seeing the glorious riot of color in Central Park that autumn. By Thanksgiving she was dead.

The medical examiner's report had listed coronary failure. How appropriate. Her heart had finally just given up.

Nine years ago now.

Linus took a long swallow of his vodka and forced himself to concentrate on the giant screen as Lee's anthrax segment replayed. Watching Lee hold up the test tube, Linus felt himself growing as angry as he had when he first heard that the powder was sugar instead of anthrax. Lee was a fool. A stupid, arrogant fool.

No one got away with making Linus Nazareth look like an ass.

Linus shook his head groggily, awakened by the noise coming from the hallway.

"Wayne?"

"Yeah, Dad. It's me."

"Come on in here, son."

Wayne stood in the library doorway, still wearing his overcoat, his hair tousled from the cutting wind outside. His eyes were red-rimmed.

"Have a good time?"

Wayne shrugged. "Okay, I guess."

"What'd you do?"

"Went out with some friends."

"Anyone I know?"

"I don't think so." His son wasn't giving up much.

"Well, I'm glad you went out and had some fun. You should do more of that, Wayne. You're young and free. You should be enjoying yourself."

"Okay, Dad. I'm going to bed now."

Linus listened to the sound of the footsteps going down

the spiral staircase. He waited a few minutes before following, the dog shuffling behind him. He passed Wayne's closed bedroom door before stopping at the other.

As Linus entered the dimly lit room, the night-duty nurse switched off the pencil light trained on the book she was reading.

"How's it going?" Linus asked, peering toward the single bed at the other side of the room. Tucked secure beneath the warm blankets, the thin form was barely visible.

"Fine, Mr. Nazareth."

What did he expect her to say? Nothing ever changed. There was never any good news to report. Seth slept here, in the room beside his brother's, day after day, month after month, year after year.

It was always the same.

What would this son have been? Linus asked himself the question that he had been asking for over two decades now. Would Seth have been a concert pianist or a football star? A writer or a doctor? A clergyman or a cop?

Would they have had a good relationship, closer than the one Linus had with Wayne? Would they have shared the same interests and passions? Would Seth have been a son Linus could be proud of?

He tried to shake away the wistful sadness. There was no use going over it again. Seth was what Seth was. Wayne was the only egg in Linus's basket.

SATURDAY

NOVEMBER 22

CHAPTER

53

When the network had decided to replace the weekend edition of *KEY to America* with cartoons, Annabelle had started watching *The Saturday Early Show* on CBS. As the kids ate their pancakes and drank their orange juice, she went to the living room and switched on the set, keeping the volume low. There would surely be coverage on the anthrax victim at KEY News, and Annabelle didn't need Thomas and Tara hearing about it on TV. When there was any explaining to be done, she herself would tell them.

Rubbing her shoulder, Annabelle sat on the couch, waiting with a heavy feeling in her chest. Sure enough, the anchor was leading with the story.

"Earlier this week, on the KEY News morning broadcast, *KEY to America,* Medical Correspondent Dr. John Lee, in what he claimed to be an example of the availability of anthrax, produced a vial of what he purported to be the deadly white powder. But tests by health officials determined that the substance was *not* anthrax, and Dr. Lee was subsequently fired by the network.

"Now, in a terrifying twist, a KEY News employee has been diagnosed with anthrax poisoning. Thirty-six-year-old Jerome Henning, a producer for *KEY to America,* lies in a New Jersey hospital in critical condition. Hospital officials have scheduled a news conference for later this morning, and police are investigating.

"At the KEY News Broadcast Center, *KEY to America* offices have been closed and employees are being tested for exposure."

The bedroom door opened. Mike, bleary-eyed, shuffled into the living room, his bathrobe open, revealing the rumpled boxer shorts and T-shirt beneath. The stubble on his face could practically be considered a beard, Annabelle thought as she looked at him. It had been over a week since he'd shaved. She knew because she had been counting the days.

"Hi, sleepyhead," she said with affection.

He grunted his response.

"We have pancakes, Daddy. Want some?" Tara called from the kitchen.

Mike didn't bother to answer.

"Mike, honey, Tara is talking to you," Annabelle urged. "Do you want some pancakes?"

"For God's sakes, Annabelle, I don't want any damned pancakes. Just leave me alone, will you please."

Last night's warm hopefulness was replaced with the

morning's cold ration of truth. One step forward, two steps back.

She could tell it was going to be another great day in the Murphy household.

CHAPTER 54

The metal folding gate that cordoned off the entrance to Station Break was down but not locked. As the Saturday morning worker pulled it up, he wondered who had forgotten to lock it the night before.

He busied himself, switching on lights, firing up the grill, and getting the coffee urns going. He started a pot of oatmeal cooking and sliced two dozen bagels. Next, he went to the walk-in refrigerator to get out the eggs and the big tub of cream cheese.

"Oh, man. Edgar!" He whistled as he saw it. He knelt down, shaking the lifeless body that lay on the frosted floor.

"Wake up, bro. Wake up," the food-service worker urged frantically while sensing full well that it was too late.

CHAPTER 55

As they took the subway uptown, the kids bounced in their seats. It was the day they had been waiting for over the last months, their trip to the Claremont Riding Academy. Children from six years on up could learn how to walk, trot, and canter their quiet beginner mounts. The horseback riding program stressed patience and concentration along with physical coordination, strength, and agility. Children also developed a sense of responsibility in caring for their animals. Annabelle mostly liked the idea that it would be fun.

When her parents had called from Florida, asking what they could give the twins for their birthdays last summer, Annabelle had suggested the lessons. They'd had to wait until now for an opening in the private instruction schedule. There was no way she wanted to disappoint them.

As she stood over the twins and hung on to the subway pole, Annabelle wished that Mike was taking them to their lessons. Once upon a time, he wouldn't have missed this. And she could have gone out to see Jerome again.

Not that it would make any difference to Jerome whether she came to visit or not. As Annabelle thought of him, she quickly wiped away the tears that formed at the inner corners of her eyes. She didn't want the kids to see how upset she was. She had to appear as normal as possible for Thomas and Tara. They'd had enough to worry about lately.

Annabelle checked her watch. Jerome's brother had taken the red-eye in from Los Angeles. He was probably at the hospital by now.

"I want a girl horse," declared Tara.

"A mare, Tara. A girl horse is a mare." Annabelle spoke loudly to be heard over the subway clatter.

"And I want a boy horse," Thomas added, following his sister's lead.

"That's a stallion, but I don't think you'd better count on that, Thomas. I think when you begin riding it's better to have a mare. They're gentler."

She watched the boy digest the information, knowing he was torn between pride and prudence.

"Don't worry, you can get a good ride from a mare," Annabelle reassured him.

With mittened hands in her gloved ones, mother and children walked the few blocks from the subway stop to the stable. As was true everywhere in Manhattan, space was tight. Like an apartment building, the barn was laid out compactly on several floors. The indoor riding ring was on the ground floor, the horses billeted in stalls upstairs and down. When they arrived, a man at the front door called through an intercom. Within a few minutes, two well-cared-for horses were escorted down ramps by grooms.

The comforting smell of the horse barn wafted through the air while Annabelle watched with pleasure and a tinge of apprehension as the twins went into the ring and began their lessons. An orange cat picked its way across the ring floor, dwarfed by the gentle horses. The children, wide-eyed and earnest, were listening to their instructors. In this moment, all felt right with the world.

"Annabelle? Annabelle. What are you doing here?"

Turning in the direction of the voice, Annabelle spotted Lauren Adams, dressed in caramel-colored jodhpurs, gleaming black leather riding boots, and a velvet-covered hard hat. Annabelle was suddenly conscious again of her four-year-old coat. One of the cuffs was actually starting to fray. She wished she had worn the fur jacket.

"Oh, hi, Lauren. How are you?"

"I'm fine. I didn't know you came here."

"The kids are starting lessons." Annabelle gestured toward the ring.

"Oh, that's nice for them. It's something they can enjoy their whole lives. I started when I was just a kid too. Even though I'm a city girl now, I come every weekend to ride on the bridal paths in the park. I never miss it. Even on a weekend like this, when my boyfriend is in town."

Annabelle had seen people riding horses in Central Park

and always thought they seemed so entitled. That was Lauren. To the manner born. Or at least she appeared to be.

"You're lucky."

"I don't know that luck has anything to do with it. I just make it a priority in my life. I need to have this time to myself. I deserve it."

What was the point in trying to explain to Lauren that the breezy observation was only small talk? Besides work, Annabelle didn't think she and Lauren had much in common, and she knew that they would never be friends.

"It's terrible about Jerome, isn't it?" Annabelle changed the subject.

"I'll say. And I think KEY News should have one big lawsuit on its hands. I'm thinking about calling in sick next week, 'til they get that place cleaned up and can guarantee me that there isn't any danger."

It's always about you, isn't it, Lauren? Annabelle thought, turning away to watch Tara and Thomas.

"Will I see you at Linus's tomorrow?" Lauren asked.

Annabelle sighed with quiet exasperation. *Linus's party. How could Linus be having a stupid party when Jerome was lying deathly ill?*

"I'm not sure yet. Is Linus even still having it?"

"Oh, yes. I spoke with him yesterday before I left the office and he's not canceling. Life must go on and all that. You should come, Annabelle. Have a little fun. I'm looking forward to it."

You might be the only one who is.

CHAPTER 56

Linus woke up late, last night's vodka producing the dull throb pulsing in his head. Walking into the master bathroom, he opened the medicine cabinet and pulled a bottle of aspirin from the shelf. He swallowed three, then grabbed his electric toothbrush and squeezed the peppermint-flavored paste on the bristles. As he brushed, he stared at the open cabinet.

Something was different. He could swear things had been moved.

He tried to recall what had been in there. The aftershave, the mouthwash, the razor, and the shaving cream all were where they should be. So were the Tums and the Viagra.

The Cipro. That was what was missing.

He had been keeping it ever since the episodes at the other networks. The pharmacist had told him that it had a three-year shelf life. He still hadn't begun taking it, nor did he intend to—unless the nasal swab indicated that he should. The side effects of the drug were said to be lousy:

vomiting, diarrhea, headaches, and dizziness. He didn't need that for sixty days.

But now, even if he needed it, the antibiotic wasn't here. Wayne must have beaten him to it. The hypochondriac.

He wished that son of his had bigger *cojones*. Wayne was such a disappointment.

CHAPTER 57

"Can we, Mommy?" asked Tara.

"Yeah, Mom, can we?" Thomas seconded.

Why not make the morning a complete success? To heck with balanced lunches and spoiled appetites. Life was short. She doubted Jerome, if he could, would look back on his life and wish that he had eaten less junk food.

"Okay," Annabelle answered.

The twins let out a collective "Yea!" as they crossed Bleecker Street to the Magnolia Bakery.

In the window of the tiny shop, a young woman spread thick icing in shades of pink, green, and yellow on top of generously sized cupcakes. Tubs of peach and blue sprinkles and candy flowers waited nearby, ready to complete the decoration. Once they were inside, sugar cookies, blueberry muffins, and cheesecakes beckoned from the glass display cases.

"I want a green cupcake," said Thomas.

"I want a pink one," his sister chimed.

Annabelle got a dozen of the chocolate drop cookies Mike liked and some of the peanut butter ones she adored and paid for the order. The kids were barely out the door when they begged not to have to wait until they got home to eat their treats.

"Let's go over to the playground for a little while," Annabelle suggested. "You can eat them there."

It didn't take much to convince them. The Bleecker Playground on Abingdon Square was one of their favorite haunts. There the three of them sat on a bench, warmed by the noonday sun, as Annabelle distributed the cupcakes from the paper bag.

Thomas struggled to peel the paper back from his cupcake.

"Take off your mittens, honey. I'll hold them for you."

The child obeyed, handing the red mittens to his mother, and she stuffed them into her coat pocket. Reaching into the bakery bag, Annabelle pulled out a cookie for herself and watched with pleasure as her children ate, the icing coating their little lips and spreading onto their rosy cheeks.

A little fun never killed anyone.

CHAPTER

58

Yelena Gregory, FBI agents, New York City Health Department officials, and police homicide detectives. Joe Connelly mentally weighed which formidable source was causing him the most *agita* as they combed through the Broadcast Center on what should have been a quiet Saturday.

Yelena was straining to keep control.

"We've never had a murder in the history of the Broadcast Center," she murmured as they watched Edgar's sheet-covered body being rolled out of the cafeteria. "And we potentially have another one out there in a hospital in New Jersey." She gave Joe a piercing stare. "KEY stock closed down yesterday. Monday will probably be worse. What are we going to do?"

"We're doing all we can, Yelena. Mostly, we have to let these professionals do their jobs."

Joe knew that the idea of sitting back and waiting didn't sit well with Yelena Gregory. She was accustomed to giving orders and having them followed with quick results. What was going on here was to a great extent out of her control, and she couldn't like that one bit.

"Everyone here is going to be looking to you, Yelena," he reminded her. "They will need to be reassured that everything is going to be all right."

The corner of Yelena's mouth lifted in a wry half smile. "How do I tell them that when I don't even know if I believe it myself?"

CHAPTER 59

Thirty-one Highland Place was abuzz with activity. Police cars flanked the HAZMAT truck parked in front of the Victorian house. Neighbors who ventured out to see what was happening were told to go back inside their homes. Both ends of the street were cordoned off to keep cars and pedestrians away.

Inside the house, men, suited and masked, methodically worked their way through the rooms where Jerome Henning lived. On the second floor, a desk drawer was opened, and a gloved hand pulled out a test tube.

A neighbor's telephone call to the news desk hot line led the Garden State News Network satellite truck to Maplewood. Unable to gain access to Highland Place, the van parked on the next block.

"Let me scope things out," ordered the reporter, leaving the truck operator and the cameraman to set up. He was trespassing, he knew, as he cut through the yard of the house that backed up to the Henning place. When he got to the row of boxwoods that separated the backyards, a policeman stopped him. PATROLMAN ANDREW KENNY was engraved on the identification badge.

"Don't go any further, bud."

"Press, Garden State News Network, Officer Kenny. But I'm just doing my job, ya know?"

"Yeah, I know, but you've got to go back."

"What can you tell me?"

"Sorry. No dice. Now get going," the officer ordered.

Trying to figure out what he would do next, the reporter turned and started to leave just as the back door of the house opened.

"Hey, Andy," came the yell. "We think we found the anthrax in the guy's desk drawer."

CHAPTER

60

Her son pulled on the mittens that had been stashed in her pocket.

"Those mittens are getting pretty ratty looking, Thomas," Annabelle said. There was a hole in the thumb section, exposing Thomas's skin. "We've got to get you a new pair."

It wouldn't even require a trip to the store. On their way home from the park, a street vendor offered a colorful array of hats, scarves, and gloves. Annabelle usually liked to stuff the kids' Christmas stockings with those types of things, but she was in her "why wait, life is short" mode. It would be nice to have the twins decked out in new scarf-and-mittens sets when they went to the parade on Thanksgiving morning.

They picked out a green-striped cap and mittens for Thomas. Tara wanted purple.

It wasn't even worth washing the old mittens and dropping them off at a Goodwill bin.

"Just throw them in that garbage can, Thomas," instructed his mother, pointing to the receptacle as they turned the corner at Perry Street.

CHAPTER 61

"I'm going to Chumley's for a beer with the guys," Mike announced.

Annabelle looked up from the laundry she was folding, noticing with pleasure that her husband had actually shaved. His hair was washed, his fingernails clipped. He wore her favorite navy crewneck sweater, which set off his blue eyes, and a pair of faded but pressed jeans. Except for the fact that his pants hung more loosely than she remembered, Mike almost looked like his old self. His old handsome self.

"You are?" she asked with surprise. Then quickly added, "That's great, honey. Have a good time."

She couldn't remember the last time Mike had gone out with his friends. Once he had cherished the camaraderie but, over the last months, he had shown so little interest in their treasured brotherhood. The guys called often to see how Mike was doing, to encourage him to come down to the firehouse to spend some time together. Mostly, Mike would refuse to come to the phone, leaving Annabelle to make lame excuses. That he wanted to go out and meet them for a beer was a good sign.

"Should I hold dinner?"

"No. I'll probably grab something there. I suddenly have a yen for one of those burgers."

Appetite. Another good sign.

He actually stopped to kiss her on the cheek before he walked out the door. With a warm feeling, Annabelle finished putting the folded clothes away. The twins were content, playing in their room with Legos, building their own unique version of a castle. Her husband had gone out to meet some of the guys for a beer. Everything felt almost normal again.

Fortified, she braced herself for a call to the hospital.

Jerome was still in critical condition.

CHAPTER 62

Gavin eyed the striking redhead who walked past the bank of amaryllis decorating the Ritz-Carlton bar. He'd like to get himself some of that.

She must have felt his eyes on her, because she turned to look at him straight on. He smiled and lifted his brandy snifter in salute. She turned away.

He took a large, quick swallow of his drink and threw a ten-dollar tip on the small table, eager to get away now. If Marguerite had let him come home, he wouldn't be in this situation. It was embarrassing. Here he was sitting in a hotel bar five blocks from Ground Zero, lusting after a woman who looked to be a good thirty years younger than he was.

Well, nobody could blame him for the last part. One minute with that wrinkled harpy Marguerite, and any man worth his salt would understand why he was forced to look elsewhere.

Screw Marguerite—and the horse she rode in on. If she was so damned worried about her own safety, he was going to see that he was very pampered in his exile. This hotel was the place to do it. He'd heard the Ritz-Carlton in Battery Park was terrific, and he had been wanting to try it out. Catering to the financial world's haute clientele, the hotel had all the amenities and then some. There was a technology butler to help with computer problems and a bath butler to draw a long, restful soak in the tub. Gavin's Art Deco–style room looked out over New York Harbor, the hotel providing a telescope in every room to get a closer look at the Statue of Liberty, Ellis Island, or even the skippers who sailed their boats into the Hudson River. The marble bathroom was stocked with thick lotions and beauty potions and the fluffiest towels. Two plush robes hung in the closet, waiting to wrap guests after the massages that could be ordered given in the room. Even those pillows last night were the most luxurious he had ever slept on.

Unfortunately, KEY News wasn't going to pick up the tab for his weekend stay in the city. He'd have to pay for it himself. But it was worth it, and he could afford it.

Standing in the elegant lobby, Gavin decided he was hungry. He'd go upstairs to the other bar, have another drink, and order something light to eat. Taking the elevator to the fourteenth floor, he got off at Rise. He chose a table near the window and settled down to admire Lady Liberty aglow in the harbor while he waited for his food.

"Gavin Winston? What are you doing here on a Saturday night?"

Gavin rose to shake his stockbroker's hand. "I could ask you the same question, Paul."

"Oh, you know, Saturday, Sunday, I'm always doing business. Are you by yourself, man?"

Gavin hesitated. He didn't want to have to invite the broker to sit down, but he couldn't see a way around it.

"What'll you have?"

"Okay, a quick one. Glenlivet, rocks."

After a few sips of the alcohol, the talk turned to Wellstone and the SEC investigation.

"Are you a little nervous, Gavin? We all are."

"You only have to be nervous, Paul, when you have something to hide."

CHAPTER 63

Beth swirled from side to side, eyeing herself in the full-length mirror that hung on the back of her closet door. She wasn't sure if she would end up wearing the new outfit tomorrow to Linus's party. The brown crushed velvet skirt was becoming, falling midcalf, elongating her form and making her look thinner, but she worried that it was too conservative for Linus's tastes. She wanted him to take notice. But, after all, it was a football party. She couldn't go prancing in there wearing cocktail attire.

Beth held her breath, sucked in her stomach, and wondered what Lauren Adams would be wearing. She always seemed to have just the right thing. It certainly did not hurt that Lauren was a perfect size 6.

Beth took off the skirt and arranged it on the bed, knowing the manicure scissors were in the vanity drawer. Taking them out, she carefully snipped the tag that was stitched on the inside of the skirt. She might be a size 16, but she didn't need to be reminded of it every time she dressed. And if, just if, her skirt was to find itself parted from her body, she didn't want to risk Linus's seeing the embarrassing double digits.

She had been trying. She really had. Going to the Weight Watchers meetings, counting her points, keeping her food journal, taking the stairs rather than the elevator. It was hard, but she knew if she could just lose the extra baggage, she could get Linus to come around, to view her as a woman, not merely his capable employee.

She had already lost ten pounds. Forty sticks of butter, the Weight Watcher leader said to visualize it. Yet there was so far to go. And now the holidays were coming. Traditionally for her, Thanksgiving kicked off a six-week eating binge. Beth didn't know how she was going to get through the season this year. She had to keep her eyes on the prize, not let herself be distracted. The long-term goal was Linus. She had to remember that.

Her stomach was growling now. She wrapped herself in a roomy robe and walked down the hallway to the small kitchen. Opening the freezer, she scanned the contents and selected a Lean Cuisine dinner. A minuscule Salisbury steak and a dollop of mashed potatoes. Five points.

While the microwave hummed, Beth made the notation in her journal and computed the points she could consume for the rest of the day. She'd have enough left for a bag of low-fat popcorn and a diet Coke when she watched TV tonight. She hoped that would be enough to fill another Saturday night alone.

The diet dinner took no time to down. As she scraped every last bit of gravy from the plastic dish, Beth wondered if a case of anthrax would lead to weight loss.

It might be worth it.

CHAPTER 64

Mike still wasn't home when Annabelle turned on the eleven o'clock news, and she was starting to be concerned. But the lead story diverted her from worry about her husband.

"People in Maplewood, New Jersey, are anxious tonight after health department officials confirmed that anthrax was found in the home of thirty-six-year-old resident Jerome Henning. Henning, a producer for KEY News, is in critical condition in Essex Hills Hospital, suffering from inhalation anthrax poisoning.

"Authorities searched Henning's home this afternoon, finding the white powder that tests showed to be anthrax. Earlier in the week, on the KEY News morning show, *KEY to America,* Medical Correspondent Dr. John Lee claimed to display anthrax. Tests on that substance indicated that it was not the deadly powder but was, instead, powdered sugar. Tests done at selected spots in KEY News offices showed no contamination, but the building is going through more extensive testing this weekend.

"Police and federal agents are trying to put the pieces of the anthrax puzzle together, along with investigating another sad twist. The body of forty-two-year-old food-service worker Edgar Rivers was found this morning in the freezer of the KEY cafeteria. Rivers had been stabbed in the back."

Annabelle listened in shock, trying to take in the enormity of the newscaster's words. She didn't know Edgar well, hadn't ever had a long conversation with him, but she'd instinctively liked him and felt happy when she saw him in the hallway or in the cafeteria. He was a familiar part of her weekday life, and the news that he had been stabbed to death not twenty feet from where they so often exchanged smiles and pleasantries left Annabelle feeling both sickened and terrified.

Edgar. The happy man who cheerfully delivered their refreshments in the morning, his smile warm and welcoming, his shirt starched and pressed, his shoes polished with care. The pride he took in his job evident for all to see. What about those sweet little boys who so clearly adored their uncle?

Who would want to hurt that poor sweet man? Was Edgar's murder somehow connected with Jerome's poisoning? Was her stolen tote bag not merely another random theft in Manhattan—did the thief know exactly what he wanted?

Annabelle sat back on the sofa, suddenly aware of the soreness in her shoulder. She grabbed the telephone to call Constance, then remembered that her friend had gone to Washington to visit her mother and wouldn't be back until Linus's party tomorrow.

She wished Mike would come home. Annabelle didn't feel good about being the only adult in the apartment tonight.

CHAPTER 65

He needed another CD holder. There was no more room on the entertainment center shelves for his ever-growing accumulation. Painstakingly filed by category—pop, jazz, country, rap—the compact discs stood side by side in an impressive music library. Russ was proud of and fanatical about his collection. But the CDs, along with the DVDs and videotapes, were taking over the apartment.

He needed more closet space too. A man on television had to have the right clothes, and he had been doing his best to separate himself from the entertainment reporters and movie critics on the competing networks. No navy blazers or bow ties for him. He'd invested a small fortune in suede, leather, and Italian silk. It bothered him every time he crammed a costly garment into his stuffed closets.

It was time to move. And now he could afford it. He was just waiting for a bigger place in the same building to become available. Or perhaps, if he was lucky, that pill in the apartment next door would decide to move. He could buy her co-op and knock through the wall, enlarging his place.

She was always complaining, that one, about the noise coming from his apartment. He played his music too loud, too late, she claimed, and she couldn't sleep. She was a coward, to boot. She never confronted him face-to-face, only slid her nasty letters of protest under his front door. He would be thrilled to see her go.

Inspired, Russ snorted a line of cocaine, slid the new Matchbox Twenty disc into the stereo, and piped up the volume. His foot tapped and he hummed to himself as he began to sort through the pile of mail. Bill, bill, bill, bill. He tossed them aside, unopened.

At the bottom of the pile, he found what he wanted. He ripped open the white envelope and smiled.

It was nice to have another steady source of income, but he'd have to be more careful in the future. With Linus on the warpath, Russ couldn't be so blatant in his praise of lackluster films.

CHAPTER 66

Annabelle lay awake with the bedroom door ajar, listening for Mike's key in the lock.

The hatch opened on the cuckoo clock the kids loved, the tiny bird chirping one time.

Annabelle toyed with the idea of calling Chumley's but resisted the impulse. Mike didn't need her checking up on him as she would on a child.

As she tossed in the double bed, her mind turned to Jerome's manuscript. She wished now that she had made it a point to read it all as soon as he'd given it to her. It would be a starting point in determining the people who might want to hurt him. But had Jerome somehow mistakenly contaminated himself? What was anthrax doing in his own house?

She would call the police tomorrow and let them know about the theft. Jerome undoubtedly had a copy of the manuscript at home; at the very least there would be one on his computer. That could help the police with their investigation.

She heard footsteps now in the hall. Annabelle switched on the bedside lamp. In the bedroom doorway, Mike swayed just a bit.

"Have fun?"

"Yeah. We had a good time." He smiled.

My God, he smiled.

"How are the guys?"

Mike pulled his sweater over his head. "You know them. They're always good for some laughs."

Not recently, thought Annabelle.

"I'm so glad, Mike. It's so good to see you happy."

I pray it lasts, she thought. She wanted to tell him about what she had seen on the news tonight and how she now suspected that the stolen manuscript might be tied somehow to Jerome's poisoning and perhaps even to Edgar's murder, but she didn't want to risk spoiling the moment.

He came over and sat on the edge of the bed. Annabelle could smell the not-unpleasant scent of beer as Mike leaned down to kiss her.

"I miss you, Annabelle."

Even if it was the beer talking, Annabelle didn't care as she closed her eyes and responded with hunger, feeling his strong arms encircle her body. It had been way too long, and she wasn't about to let this opportunity slip by.

It was an affirmation of life, and she needed that.

SUNDAY

NOVEMBER 23

CHAPTER

67

After the eight o'clock Mass at St. Patrick's Cathedral, Beth knelt on the padded kneeler at the shrine to the Blessed Mother and lit a candle. She thought of Jerome and supposed she should light another one for him, but she couldn't bring herself to do it. Jerome had been the beginning of her downward spiral. She knew that forgiving him would be the Christian thing to do, but she couldn't.

Nor could she forgive herself.

The light flickered behind the red glass votive as it did every Sunday. Beth stared at the flame and prayed for the unborn.

The baby would be seven years old now.

Still, she went over in her mind how she could ever have done it. She hadn't wanted to, but she was weak and too worried about what people would say. Her mother would have been devastated to think that a daughter of hers would have found herself in such a predicament. Beth couldn't face telling her mother that she was pregnant by a man who had no intention of marrying her.

She should have stood up to Jerome and insisted on having the baby, with him or without him. Even if she had not kept the child after the birth, there were so many people who would willingly have adopted her infant, thrilled by the prospect of parenthood, aching to give a child every advantage, swaddling the baby in love.

What did it matter that the child had been conceived in desperation? She'd known that Jerome was merely using her to get over Annabelle, but she'd hoped that a baby would tie him to her. It had done just the opposite. Afterward, he wanted nothing to do with her, avoiding her whenever he could.

But, in the end, she was the one who had gone ahead and had the procedure done. It was her responsibility, and the guilt of it was more than she could bear.

She had no right even setting foot in this church. She was a murderer.

CHAPTER 68

This was so unlike Clara. She was always waiting patiently outside her garden apartment when Evelyn stopped to pick her up for church. Every Sunday morning, like clockwork, Clara stood in her best clothes at the curb, not wanting to trouble her friend to have to come inside to get her. The rest of the week, Clara may have worn old slacks and sweaters as she cleaned other people's houses, but on the Lord's Day, she wore her very finest as she went to pray and give thanks to God.

Evelyn checked her watch. If Clara didn't get out here soon they were going to be late. Not that Evelyn minded all that much, but Clara enjoyed being in the pew in time to sing the processional hymn. In her thick Polish accent, she'd sing her heart out, strong and clear.

Snow fell on the windshield, and Evelyn switched on the wipers. Maybe Clara had been too cold and had gone inside to wait. Evelyn craned to look up at the window of her friend's apartment. There was no one looking down from behind the lace-trimmed glass.

Evelyn opened the car door, feeling a rush of cold air bite into her nylon-covered legs. She should have worn slacks. But she knew Clara thought women should wear dresses to church, and Evelyn humored her conservative friend.

In the vestibule of the building, Evelyn pressed the button for Clara's apartment. Once, twice, three times.

Clara would have called if she was going away or doing something out of the ordinary. Any outing was a big deal for her, and she carefully planned the slightest deviation in her schedule. *Where was she?*

Evelyn was concerned now. What if Clara was in the apartment but unable to answer the buzzer? Maybe she had fallen in the tub or something and had hit her head. Maybe someone had broken in and hurt her. Clara lived by herself. No one would know if anything was wrong inside those tidy rooms.

It was up to Evelyn to make sure that Clara was all right.

She tracked down the super, told him of her worries, and asked him to open the door.

"Maybe we should call the police," he suggested.

"Let's not waste time," Evelyn urged. "They'll just have to find you to open the door anyway."

In the Catholic church two miles away, the processional hymn concluded while, on the other side of town, Evelyn and the superintendent discovered Clara's stiff, lifeless body.

CHAPTER 69

The kids came in to wake their parents.

"It's snowing, Mommy!" Tara announced with excitement.

"Can we get our sleds out from the storage room?" Thomas hopped next to the bed.

Annabelle kept her eyes shut, not wanting to wake up, remembering why she had slept so soundly. She reached out and felt Mike beside her.

"Come on, Mommy. Get up."

For children, snow was like Christmas morning, exciting and magical and breathtaking. What happened over the years? Now Annabelle equated snow with boots and snow-suits and soggy mittens that had to be dried out. *You need an attitude adjustment, girl,* she thought as she began to roll out of the bed.

"Stay there, honey. I'll get up."

Was this already Christmas morning? Mike was pulling on his robe and stuffing his feet into moccasins.

"I'm in the mood for some French toast and sausage.

How about you, guys?" He clapped his hands, and the twins trotted after him, but not before looking at their mother for reassurance. They may have been young, but they were aware enough to sense that this was not the father they had known for the last few months. This was the old Daddy again, and they weren't sure if they could trust that yet. Annabelle didn't want to get her hopes up too high either.

Let's just take it one step at a time, she told herself, remembering Mike snapping at her the morning before. It had taken a long time for him to get into the dark place. The road out could be bumpy.

For a while, Annabelle lay under the warm comforter, inhaling the aroma of the sausage that sizzled in the kitchen and listening to the happy chatter of the twins. She could readily stay here in the snug apartment all day, the snow falling silently on the street outside. She didn't want to go to the party this afternoon. She didn't want to get up and face what she knew she must.

Annabelle decided it would be best to get it over with and begin by calling Joe Connelly. Joe could tell her who to contact in police enforcement about the stolen manuscript. She called the Broadcast Center switchboard and asked to be connected with Security, thinking that she could ask the duty person to call Joe at home and request that he call her. But the security chief answered the phone himself. "Connelly here."

"Joe, it's Annabelle Murphy from *KTA*."

"Sure, Annabelle. What's up?"

She recounted her story. The manuscript and its theft. "Jerome wasn't pulling any punches, Joe. I read just a little of it, but the parts I did get to were quite revealing. Brutal, actually. If Jerome had written about me that way, I know that I wouldn't have been happy. I'm just wondering if this is somehow tied in to the anthrax poisoning and maybe even Edgar's murder."

"You're absolutely right, Annabelle. The police and the FBI should know about this. I'll call them. I'm sure they'll want to speak with you."

CHAPTER 70

The caterer had already arrived with the party food. A large spiral-cut ham, beef tenderloin sliced for sandwiches on crusty French bread, hot potato salad, spicy chili, cheesy nachos, and cases of cold beer and wine. Forget the vegetables and tossed green salads. This was an occasion for real food and hearty appetites.

Linus was in the kitchen watching the catering staff set up when the telephone rang. He grimaced as the caller identified himself.

"Oh, hi, John," he answered with no enthusiasm in his voice.

"All ready for the party, Linus?"

"Getting there."

There was a pause before the former medical correspondent blurted, "This is a tad awkward, Linus, but I just wanted to make sure that I was still welcome."

Linus didn't skip a beat. "This is awkward for me too, John, but under the circumstances, I think you'll agree that it's better all around if you don't come to the party."

Lee's voice rose. "I can't believe it, Linus. You're hanging me out to dry. We were in this thing together and now you're leaving me twisting in the wind."

"I don't like being made a fool of, John. You know that."

"How do you think I feel? I'm a laughingstock. A laughingstock that no one is going to want to hire. And if it turns out they can trace the anthrax that infected Henning to the lab I shot at—and therefore to me—I am going to have legal problems big time."

"Those are your problems, John. Not mine."

"Well, they'll be your problems, Linus, if I tell Yelena that you knew full well what I was going to do."

Linus's mind spun as he took a slice of ham from a silver tray and popped it into his mouth. He walked out of the kitchen, out of earshot of the party workers.

"I wouldn't do that, John. Not if you have any desire to work in this business again," he warned. "I have friends, and when this whole thing dies down, I might be able to help you find another broadcasting job. But pull me into this and you're on your own. I'll make sure that no one will want to touch you."

CHAPTER 71

They were going to do an autopsy on poor Clara.

Evelyn knew her friend wouldn't like that, but she also knew that she could do nothing to stop it.

She drove home slowly over the slippery road. Everything looked so beautiful and clean, the giant gray trees covered in white, the lawns blanketed in soft powder. Clara would have enjoyed this early storm. Clara loved the snow.

Taking her hand off the steering wheel, Evelyn wiped a tear from the corner of her eye. She couldn't stand the silence in the car. Silence where Clara's animated conversation should have been. Evelyn turned on the radio.

"Jingle Bells" already. *Ridiculous.* She switched to another station. The news report was in progress.

"The anthrax victim, thirty-six-year-old Jerome Henning, is employed at KEY News. Henning is in critical condition."

Henning. That was the man Clara worked for. She talked about him all the time. He was the one who was always giving Clara tickets to things. The one she thought should have a wife and children.

If Mr. Henning had been infected with anthrax, could Clara have been poisoned too?

When I get home, I am going to call the police, Evelyn thought, just as her car began its skid into the telephone pole.

CHAPTER 72

The snowsuits were zipped and the boots wedged on. Annabelle tied a scarf around each child's neck and adjusted their ski caps. Mike was taking the twins outside to make a snowman.

Annabelle wasn't going to press her luck by trying to talk Mike into going to the party later. That he was taking the kids out to play in the snow was enough to be thankful for today. Annabelle had already called Mrs. Nuzzo to say that she needn't come to baby-sit while Mike stayed holed up inside their bedroom. He'd announced that he would be just fine with Thomas and Tara while she went to the party. And it was a bonus to be able to save a few bucks.

"Have a good time, you three," Annabelle called after them as she closed the apartment door. She rested against the back of the door, knowing exactly what she wanted to do with this quiet respite. She put water in the kettle and set it to boil before going to get a pad of paper and a pen. Then she sat at the kitchen table and began to write in outline form.

Recollections of Jerome Henning's Manuscript

1. Linus Nazareth
   —Executive Producer, *KTA*
   —Ego-driven and mean-spirited, consumed with ambitions for his broadcast
   —Willing to use anyone and anything in his quest for higher ratings
   —Examples of vicious browbeatings inflicted by Nazareth on the *KTA* staff
2. Wayne Nazareth, Linus's son
   —Associate Producer on the broadcast
   —Haunted by a childhood accident that left his twin in

a vegetative state. Jerome had done research in old local newspaper accounts of the accident.

—After he'd flunked out of college twice, his father gave Wayne a job at *KTA*. Still lives at home with his dad, and the picture painted by Jerome was pretty pathetic.

The kettle let out a shrill whistle. Annabelle got up, poured the steaming water over a tea bag, then returned to her outline, pulling further from memory.

3. Lauren Adams
   —Lifestyle Correspondent
   —Portrayed as having lots of style but little substance
   —Gunning for Constance Young's spot as host of the show and flirting with Nazareth as her way to land the job
4. Gavin Winston
   —Business Correspondent
   —Pompous, uptight, and disgusted that Nazareth is so gauche. Longs for the old ways, the more gentlemanly days of broadcasting
   —Lecherous behavior, coming on to every intern who walks in the door
   —Veiled suggestions that he may be making money on the side, through his Wall Street connections

5. John Lee
   —Medical Correspondent
   —Self-interested and self-serving
   —Trying to make himself a "personality" and parlay his national TV visibility into book deals and even bigger contract at next negotiation

Jerome hit the nail on the head with that portrait, thought Annabelle as she paused and recalled all the time Lee spent wheeling and dealing on the telephone while it fell to her to do most of the work in getting his pieces together.

6. Russ Parrish
   —Entertainment Correspondent
   —Grew up poor, but has grown to love the good life—acquired a cocaine addiction along the way
   —Thrives on going to concerts and movie openings, and hordes the freebies that come to the office

Sipping her tea, Annabelle looked over her outline, wishing again that she had read more of the manuscript. She would type the outline up in the office tomorrow and then send it on to the police. Perhaps none of these people had anything to do with the deadly chaos at KEY. But she had a responsibility to tell the police everything she knew. They needed all the help they could get to solve this nightmare.

CHAPTER

73

"My finger hurts, Daddy."

Thomas had taken off his soggy mitten and was holding his pink-skinned hand up for his father to see. Mike took the small hand and inspected it, kissing the tiny cut on the index finger.

"It's just a little cut, Thomas. It will be all right. We'll put some Bactine and a bandage on it when we get home. Do you remember how you cut it?"

The boy nodded solemnly. "In art class. We were cutting out feathers for our turkeys. I cut it on the side of the paper."

"Well, don't worry, son. It's just a little cut. The cold snow must have opened it up, but it will be all right. You'll see."

Father and children went back to building their snowman.

CHAPTER 74

"Want me to come with you to LaGuardia?" Lauren offered, hoping he wouldn't take her up on it.

"No, that's silly, angel. We'll say good-bye here."

She watched as he packed the rest of his toiletries into his kit, relieved that he could get only this afternoon flight back to Chicago. If the evening flights hadn't been fully booked, she would have had either to skip the party or to bring him with her. Neither option was acceptable. Lauren wanted to work this party alone.

"Thank goodness it will only be for a few days, sweetheart. Then we'll be together again on Thanksgiving." Lauren kissed him on the back of the neck.

He turned and took her in his arms, longing in his intelligent blue eyes. Yes, she had him right where she wanted him. But she wanted Linus as well. Not in the same lustful way that she craved her handsome investment banker, but she desired the executive producer nonetheless. Power was a tremendous aphrodisiac. Linus had the power to catapult her career.

Once she was safely ensconced in Constance Young's spot, she could drop Linus if she chose. He wouldn't be able to fire her then for fear she would shout sexual harassment. He would look like a fool. And if Lauren was sure of anything, she was sure of that. Linus would do anything to avoid looking foolish.

CHAPTER 75

Bringing a bottle of good wine to Linus's party was like bringing coals to Newcastle, but Gavin wouldn't think of coming empty-handed. Certain things were expected. That was the way he was raised. He was also raised to be prompt. Being on time was a sign of respect. Thus, he was the first to arrive.

Though he had been here each autumn for many years, he was still impressed as he walked into the penthouse apartment. Three floors on Central Park West. Twelve million at least. Linus was well paid, but KEY hadn't afforded him this place. This was the direct result of marrying well. Very well.

Wayne met him at the thirty-first-floor entry.

"Dad's still in the shower. Come on up and have a drink."

They walked through the spacious family room and climbed the spiral staircase to the main floor of the apartment. A beautifully proportioned corner living-dining area offered spectacular views of New York from the oversize thermal-paned windows. Central Park and the lake straight ahead, the city skyline towering to the south, the Jacqueline Kennedy Onassis Reservoir lying north.

"This must have been a great place to watch the Thanksgiving parade when you were young," Gavin observed, looking down at Central Park West.

"Not as good as you might think," answered Wayne. "We're up so high, we'd only see the tops of the balloons. Santa Claus was a little red-and-white blur."

A waiter approached and took Gavin's drink order.

"Mrs. Winston wasn't able to make it?" asked Wayne, grasping for small talk, wishing his father would finish getting dressed and come out here.

"No, she wasn't feeling well," Gavin lied. Marguerite detested coming to office functions, and Gavin was just as glad. Especially this time. Let her sit up there in Connecticut and pet her precious pooch.

The bell rang, and Wayne excused himself to greet the next guest.

He was feeling miserable. His head ached, and he grabbed the railing as he walked down the spiral staircase, steadying himself. This Cipro really packed a punch. Wayne had been back and forth to the bathroom all day, not knowing whether to bend over the bowl or sit on it.

How was he going to get through this party?

Maybe, as soon as more guests came, he could slip away without anyone noticing. He could hole up in his bedroom and nobody would even realize that he was gone.

Sometimes, twisted as he knew it was, Wayne actually envied his brother. Seth lay in bed in his safe room, day after day, his needs well tended to. Fed, warmed, bathed. His hair was cut for him, his nails clipped. His pajamas were made of the softest cottons, his blankets the softest wools. Music was piped in to soothe him, though only God knew if Seth needed soothing. Wayne doubted it.

Seth didn't have to worry about what he was going to do with his life or what other people thought of him. He didn't have to be concerned about his professional or personal reputation. No one expected anything of Seth. His father was never disappointed in him.

Wayne hated himself when he thought like this. Seth never saw a glowing sunrise or a hot orange sunset. He'd never kissed a woman or chugged an icy beer. Never driven a car, letting a warm summer breeze blow through the open window while the radio blared, tapping his hand on the steering wheel to the beat. He'd missed baseball and soccer and football games and summer camp and pony rides and birthday parties and all the little things that happened every single day. Spicy hot dogs and crisp french fries, kites flying high above Central Park, sledding through the snow, jumping through the waves. He had missed his life.

But he'd also never caught their mother weeping time after time as she'd sat beside his bed. Seth hadn't had to interpret the haunted, anguished expression on his father's face when he came into the room to check on his fallen son. He didn't have to keep trying to make it up to them for everything. He didn't have to fail miserably.

Nor did Seth have to live with any guilt about what might have been.

Wayne pasted a smile on his face, opening the door to welcome the next person to the party.

CHAPTER 76

"There's a lasagna in the refrigerator. Just stick it in the oven and heat it up, okay, Mike?"

"Don't worry, Annabelle. Don't worry, we'll be fine. Go and have a good time."

He had been more active today than he had in a long time, and Annabelle thought he looked tired now. Giving the twins dinner and their baths could leave him exhausted. She didn't want to leave him, but she had to go to this damned party.

"Mrs. Nuzzo's number is on the bulletin board. Don't hesitate to call her if you need help, honey."

"Annabelle," he said with exasperation, "I'm fine."

"I know you are, sweetheart, I know you are." She kissed him on the cheek and pulled on the beaver jacket. "Tara, Thomas, I'm going now," she called.

The children scurried from the bedroom and hugged her good-bye.

"You look pretty, Mommy," declared Thomas.

"Thank you, kind sir." Annabelle laughed, hugging the little boy, knowing that her hair was being mussed by the small arms wrapped around her neck, but not caring. "You two, be good for Daddy." She turned to her husband. "I won't be late, and I'm on my cell phone if you need me."

CHAPTER 77

Now *this* is where he should be looking for a place.

Russ stood on the sidewalk and looked up at the cantilevered terraces on the towering Majestic. Those were a far cry from the tiny porches affixed to the old row house back in Baltimore.

He hated going back there, but he would have to this week. There was no way around it. He had promised, and his mother was counting on his visit. She was already cooking for it.

But he had prepared her for the fact that he wasn't going to spend the night. Driving down Thursday morning after the show, a quick visit, and then driving back up to New York that night. He had a review due Friday.

Mother didn't need to know that the review would be pretaped. Let her think he was doing it live in the studio. She wouldn't be able to discern the difference. The average viewer couldn't either.

No, on Friday, Russ would be out in the Hamptons, enjoying the weekend hospitality of a movie studio executive. No matter that it would be cold out there. He'd heard the guy had a fabulous home. Lots of space and giant glass walls that offered awesome views of the Atlantic. A staff that catered to every whim. A chance to spend quality time discussing potential business opportunities.

If all went well, Linus might have a new neighbor.

CHAPTER 78

His lawyer might have taken weekends off, but the FBI sure didn't.

"I won't say anything without my attorney, and I won't be able to reach him until tomorrow."

John Lee used all his concentration to stay calm. Federal agents hovering in one's home, insinuating that one was going to be implicated in anthrax poisoning, were enough to terrify anyone. But he couldn't panic.

"Your confederate at the lab has admitted now that he gave you the anthrax to smuggle out. You yourself boasted of it on national television. Of course, we have the whole thing on videotape," Special Agent McGillicuddy declared. "Now, anthrax has one of your coworkers in critical condition, and it's a good bet that he isn't going to make it. Yes, Dr. Lee, I suggest you do call your lawyer."

"But the tube I displayed only had sugar in it," Lee protested. "And I heard on the news that they found a container of anthrax in Jerome Henning's house. He could have poisoned himself."

"We'll see, Dr. Lee. That material is being tested further. They'll be able to determine if that anthrax is the same strain as the one you got from the lab. This would be a good time for you to cooperate, before anyone dies."

Special Agent Lyons stared into the physician's eyes. "Tell us why Jerome Henning had that anthrax, Dr. Lee. Were you and Henning in cahoots on this?"

Lee cleared his throat and swallowed. This shouldn't go any further. He walked to the front door and opened it.

"Please leave now. I have nothing more to say until I have a chance to talk to my attorney."

CHAPTER 79

Beth eyed the tray of cheesy nachos and debated in her mind. Were a few delicious bites worth all those points? They just might be.

"Cheese is the fat man's candy." Her Weight Watchers

leader's dictum ran through Beth's head as she passed on the nachos and searched in vain for a vegetable platter. This party was going to be a challenge. Everything Linus was serving was so caloric. She should have eaten before she came.

Linus wasn't paying her a bit of attention. He was talking to everyone else, regaling them with his stories. How could she draw him into conversation?

Football. Linus loved football. While Beth couldn't have had less interest in what she considered a brutal sport, a bunch of big men fighting viciously for a silly brown ball, she had made it a point to read the sports section this morning for some insight on the game. The New York Giants were playing the Houston Texans. Linus should be happy, as the Giants were favored to win.

Beth waited for her opportunity. When Linus went to get another beer, she snagged him. "The Giants really need to control the ball and the clock and keep their defense off the field, don't you think, Linus?"

"You're right." He seemed impressed at her observation. "And they have to run that damned thing."

But he couldn't have been too impressed, and he definitely didn't want to engage Beth in further conversation. He had turned and made a beeline for the staircase, where Lauren Adams was making her grand entrance.

She looks like Audrey Hepburn, Beth thought as she viewed with envy the pencil-thin figure in the simple black dress.

Lauren had swept her hair up into a French twist. All she needed was the cigarette holder and the long gloves, and the look would have been complete.

Linus was fawning over her.

Beth went to find the nachos.

CHAPTER 80

Sipping her glass of Chablis, Annabelle observed Beth Terry's sad gaze. It was obvious to the people in the office that Beth had a thing for Linus. And just as obvious that Linus couldn't have cared less about his unit manager, except to the extent that she benefited *KTA*.

She felt sorry for Beth. Though she hadn't been around for it, and Jerome had never spoken of it to her, Annabelle had heard about Beth's involvement with Jerome, how he had dated her right after Annabelle married Mike. Very rarely did anybody get away with keeping office romances private at KEY News, and social histories were often recounted in whispers.

Annabelle suspected that, when things ended with

Jerome, Beth hadn't taken it well. Annabelle remembered Beth as having been quite thin then. All the weight she had put on suggested lots of comfort eating.

Had Jerome written about Beth in his manuscript? she wondered.

Annabelle hoped not. It was one thing to put down on paper events that happened in a professional setting. It was quite another, and despicable, to reveal the most personal things that occurred between a man and a woman.

CHAPTER 81

At Essex Hills Hospital, Jerome Henning was not alone.

His brother and two nurses stood beside his hospital bed as the doctor switched off the ventilator.

Time of death: 5:34 P.M.

CHAPTER 82

During the halftime show, Linus decided that he should be the center of attention.

"I have a little surprise for everyone," he announced. "Everybody gets an advance copy of *The "Only" Thing: Winning the TV News Game,* hot off the presses."

The guests murmured and applauded politely. As the paperbacks were handed out, Constance elbowed Annabelle. "Oh, goodie. Linus's book instead of an end-of-the-year bonus."

Linus's face grinned from the front of the book. Annabelle stroked the glossy cover. "Sure, I'd much rather have this than extra money, wouldn't anybody?" she whispered back.

The party guests began leafing through the pages, looking for their own names and for those of their colleagues.

"What a crock."

Annabelle turned toward the inebriated Gavin Winston, who had come up behind her.

"Shh," she warned, holding her finger to her mouth.

Gavin waved her off. "Ah, he won't hear me," he said, nodding in the executive producer's direction. "He's too busy strutting around like a peacock." Gavin held the book open to the introduction and began to read, slurring slightly. "I'm a television guy, so the idea of writing a book was a daunting one. But it's been my pleasure to write this book. Every single word of it brought so many vivid memories flooding back."

Gavin hiccuped. "Pardon me, Annabelle. But let me tell you something. If Linus wrote this book himself, I'm Marie Antoinette."

CHAPTER 83

Yelena was exhausted. She'd hardly slept the last several nights, and she just wanted to have a drink, take a warm bath, and forget about her problems for a little while. She didn't want to go to the party, but she knew Linus would be insulted if she didn't attend. The thought of his dog slobbering on her was more than she could bear right now.

The hell with him. Linus would just have to understand.

She was pouring herself a scotch when Joe Connelly called. The poor guy hadn't left the Broadcast Center all weekend.

"What's up, Joe?" she asked wearily.

"I'm afraid I have more bad news, Yelena. Jerome Henning died. It looks like we may have two homicides on our hands now."

CHAPTER 84

"Look, kids," Mike bargained. "If you take your baths now, you can watch Disney before you go to bed."

It worked. He left Thomas and Tara soaking in the tub with the bathroom door open while he went about cleaning up the dinner mess. He wanted Annabelle to come home to a clean apartment. He felt a bit like a kid himself, wanting her to be proud of him. And, truth be told, it felt good to be doing something productive for a change. It felt good to *want* to do something.

If this was the medication talking—and it must be, since

nothing else had changed—Mike was going to keep on taking it. Not that he had stopped worrying about the things that had been bothering him over the last months, but now the sharp edges seemed to be smoother. The unbearable, bearable. The burden, somehow lifted.

Better living through pharmaceuticals. For today at least. He'd have to take it one day at a time and hope for the best.

He went back to the bathroom and helped the twins get dried off and into their pajamas.

"Don't forget, Daddy. I need more Bactine on my boo-boo."

The antiseptic was sprayed on the small finger. Mike applied a colorful bandage at Thomas's insistence.

"There you go, Sport. All set."

"I love you, Daddy." Thomas threw his arms around Mike's waist.

"I love you too, son." He bent to kiss the child on the top of the head. "I love you too."

The microwave beeped. Mike pulled open the popcorn bag and emptied its contents into a large ceramic bowl. The twins were delighted as he set the bowl on the coffee table before them.

"It's just like going to the movies, Daddy," Tara observed.

"Even better. You can wear your pajamas, and there's no tall guy in front of you blocking your view." Mike squeezed in between the kids on the sofa.

Just as the Disney theme music began to play, the telephone rang.

"Bummer," he whispered, getting up to go to the kitchen to answer.

"Annabelle Murphy, please," said a man's voice.

"She's not here right now. Who's calling?"

"This is Peter Henning."

"Oh yes, Peter. I'm Mike. Annabelle's husband. How is your brother doing?"

The man's voice was flat as he delivered the news. "Jerome passed away an hour and a half ago."

CHAPTER 85

Linus watched Lauren's desirable behind slither up the spiral staircase to the thirty-third floor. He followed, eager to be alone with her.

The library had high ceilings and opened up to a large

decked terrace with stunning views of Central Park and the skyline, extending east over the park, west over the Hudson, and south all the way to New York Harbor.

If that display, and what it implied, didn't turn Lauren on, nothing would.

Oh, God. Something's wrong with the kids, thought Annabelle as she felt her cell phone vibrate. *Please, Mike, be all right.* She flipped the phone open.

"What's wrong?" she asked, straining to hear over the din of the party. "Hold on a minute. I can't hear you." She walked to the bathroom and closed the door behind her.

"I'm sorry to call you at the party, honey, but I knew you'd want to know. Jerome's brother just called. Jerome's dead, Annabelle."

Yelena's car dropped her off in front of the Majestic. This was the responsible thing to do. She must tell the troops in person about their colleague's death.

As she was riding up the elevator, her cell phone rang.

It was Joe Connelly again. This time, with test results.

"They only found traces of anthrax in one spot. The rest of the offices are clear."

"Where was it?" the news president asked.

"In Annabelle Murphy's office."

CHAPTER 86

John Lee sat in his apartment, staring blankly at the television screen. He didn't know who was winning or losing the game, and he didn't care. All Lee was sure of was that he didn't intend to be left holding the bag alone.

Linus had known all about the anthrax plan, and it wasn't fair that he was denying it now, making the medical correspondent the goat.

Seething with anger, the doctor clicked off the TV.

Unwelcome or not, he was going to the party.

CHAPTER

87

Annabelle supposed Linus should be the first to know about Jerome's death. But she couldn't find her boss. She had just told Constance the news when she spotted Yelena taking off her coat.

"Yelena. I have to talk with you."

"And I you, Annabelle," said Yelena, eyeing the Irish setter she hoped to avoid. "Let's go somewhere private."

There had been three people waiting to use the bathroom when Annabelle exited after taking the call from Mike. So that venue was out. The game roared on the television set in the living area, and the kitchen was full of activity.

"Downstairs?" Annabelle suggested.

Yelena nodded and followed Annabelle down the spiral staircase.

There was no one in the family room. Yelena excused herself and blew her nose in a tissue she took from her handbag.

"Cold?" asked Annabelle.

"No, allergies. But it's nothing. What did you want to talk to me about?"

"Jerome's brother called. Jerome died a little while ago."

"I know. The hospital told the police, who informed Joe Connelly. I'm sorry, Annabelle. I know you two were"—Yelena paused—"friends."

So Yelena knew that she and Jerome had been involved once. Annabelle wasn't surprised. The trusty office gossip mill rarely failed.

"Yes, we were." She felt the tears coming.

Yelena reached out and patted Annabelle's hand. "I'm sorry to have to tell you this, but I have more bad news."

What else? What else could there be? Annabelle felt her throat constrict as she waited for Yelena to continue.

"Traces of anthrax were found in your office, Annabelle."

Annabelle watched Yelena go back up the stairs.

She mustn't panic.

Her first thoughts were about the kids and Mike. Thank God, the contamination was in the office, miles away from their apartment. She had already been tested, and the health department would have called her immediately if she had come up positive. She had to stay calm, but she wanted to go home.

Where had they put the coats?

She walked out of the family room, down the hallway to the first door. An empty bedroom. Then on to the next.

"Oh, I'm sorry. Please, excuse me."

"It's all right, Annabelle. You can come in."

Wayne was sitting on a chair next to the bed.

"I was just giving the nurse a break," he explained.

Annabelle nodded, wanting to get away from the sight of the tortured young man and his ruined twin. Should she tell him about Jerome? If she didn't tell Wayne, he would think it odd, and he might be hurt if he realized she hadn't included him in the sad news that, by now, was spreading through the party upstairs.

"Wayne, Jerome just passed away," she said softly.

He didn't look surprised, or particularly upset, she thought, and she'd expected a more sensitive response than the one Wayne uttered.

"I'll be all right. I'm taking my Cipro."

CHAPTER 88

Yelena's annoyance grew as she searched the penthouse.

Some host Linus was. Where was he when she needed him? The *KTA* staffers were looking to them for leadership. Together, they should make some sort of statement to the group, assuring them that all would eventually work out. A dead colleague, a contaminated office, and another murder inside the Broadcast Center had to be addressed. *Damn it.* Where was he?

All that was left was the upstairs floor.

She climbed the stairs and knocked on the closed door.

No answer.

Yelena turned the brass handle, her eyes adjusting to the dimness. Yet the light from the Manhattan skyline provided just enough illumination to see what she sorely wished she hadn't.

Linus pulled himself up from Lauren's body as she hastily attempted to cover herself with her arms.

"Get dressed, will you please?" snapped Yelena. "We have work to do."

CHAPTER 89

Dr. Lee arrived just in time to stand at the back of the room and listen to Yelena's and Linus's assurances.

"There is no need to panic. Everyone is safe."

"Everything that can be done is being done."

"Law enforcement will get to the bottom of this."

Gavin Winston called out, "Just like they did with the anthrax at CBS, NBC, and ABC?"

"Those cases were different," Yelena answered, trying to keep the anger out of her voice. "The anthrax was mailed into those networks. They couldn't determine the source. In our case, we think Jerome was exposed to the anthrax that Dr. Lee brought into the Broadcast Center."

Lee shrank back against the wall, relieved that all eyes were focused on Yelena.

"What's the difference where it came from?" piped up Russ Parrish. "If it's there, it's there. Through the mail or through the front door, it's just as deadly."

"All of the offices have been thoroughly tested, Russ." Yelena's voice was firm. "Anthrax was detected in just one area, in Annabelle's office. It's being thoroughly cleaned as we speak."

Eyes searched the room for Annabelle. She stood at the top of the staircase, fur jacket on, ready to say her good-byes. The expressions on most of her colleagues' faces read "better you than me." A few seemed to look at her with suspicion.

"Well, I think we should all be put on Cipro," Lauren declared. "We shouldn't be taking any chances."

The crowd murmured approval.

"Cipro will be provided to anyone who wants it," Yelena said with resignation. "That being the case, there is no need for anyone to avoid coming to work."

It was very interesting, almost amusing, to observe these people, who made their living in a fact-based business, become irrational. The party guests were leaving en masse, threatened and threatening.

"I'll tell you one thing. If I get anthrax, KEY is going to have one helluva lawsuit on its hands."

"If you live to bring it," came the gallows-humor response.

Another voice called. "Good-bye, Annabelle. You take care of yourself, okay?"

"Don't worry about me. I'll be fine. See you in the morning."

Hadn't the spores taken hold by now, doing their malignant work in her pink lungs? When was Annabelle going to start showing the symptoms?

MONDAY
NOVEMBER 24

CHAPTER

90

Mike slept through the alarm but was awakened by the sound of Annabelle tripping in the dark over the shoes she had left strewn on the floor the night before.

"Sorry, honey. I didn't mean to wake you," she whispered.

Their eyes adjusted to the light as he switched on the bedside lamp.

"I can't believe you're going to work," he said, squinting at her.

"What am I supposed to do, Mike?" she pleaded. "Yelena made it very clear last night that everyone was expected to be in today."

"Everyone else has an anthrax-free office."

"So? I'm supposed to stay home? I have no excuse. There's nothing physically wrong with me."

"You're so sure of that?"

"If my swab had come back positive, I'd have heard

about it. But if it will make you feel any better, I'll call this morning and make sure."

Mike was probably right. At the very least, she should reassure him. She should alleviate his worries as much as possible. He was doing better, and she didn't want to upset that applecart.

"Yeah. It would make me feel better. And I think you should go for the Cipro too."

Annabelle groaned. "That stuff's no joke, Mike, and I don't need headaches, nausea, and diarrhea."

"Better that than anthrax poisoning, my love."

CHAPTER 91

Annabelle had been here many times over the years. When she was a little girl, her mother would take her to the Easter Show and Annabelle would watch the glamorous dancers and dream, like so many other little girls, of someday being a Rockette herself. This year she already had the tickets to take her own children to the Christmas Spectacular. But no matter how many times she entered the cavernous auditorium of Radio City Music Hall, Annabelle was blown away by the majesty of the place.

Though it was 5:00 A.M., all the lights were on, illuminating the stage for the Rockettes' flawless choreography. Technicians and cameramen were setting up to record the performance. Annabelle searched the auditorium for the unit manager. She spotted Beth at the side of the stage and approached her.

"I'm here, Beth."

Beth looked up from her clipboard. "Annabelle, good. I was worried you were going to call in sick too."

"What? Who's called in?"

"A good third of the staff, including Gavin and Lauren. Linus is trying to figure out what we're going to fill their segments with now."

So the effects of the anthrax scare are being felt, thought Annabelle. She had been tempted to call in sick herself, but she hadn't wanted to look like a wimp. Though, if anyone had a reason to be worried, she supposed, it was she. After all, the others hadn't had anthrax found in *their* offices.

Sitting in one of the chairs at the back of the theater, Russ rehearsed the facts in his mind.

One million people from fifty states would attend the

Christmas Spectacular, making it the number-one live show in America. Twenty-five hundred pounds of artificial snow would fall on the stage during the run of the show.

Russ had two segments now instead of one, thanks to Gavin's and Lauren's no-shows this morning. Not that he minded the extra airtime, but he liked having more notice, more time to prepare. Being thrown into a segment left Russ unnerved, though he wasn't going to admit that to anyone. The newshounds prided themselves on their ability to ad-lib when the situation called for it, and they disdained anyone who clutched when the pressure was on.

The pressure was on, all right. Jerome was dead, and so was the poor guy from the cafeteria. Linus was in a particularly foul mood and watching for Russ to screw up. Russ ached for a little snort of his own soft, white powder.

After the show. He hoped he could hold on until then.

Damn it, he could thank Jerome for getting him hooked on the cocaine to begin with, offering it to him at a party, telling him the feeling would be stupendous. The feeling was just that—so good that Russ craved more and more and more.

Yes, Jerome had gotten Russ started on the addictive cocaine, but Jerome had gotten his comeuppance, hadn't he?

CHAPTER 92

The alarm rang again. Lauren rolled over and felt for the clock. She had been able to grab some more sleep after getting up earlier to call in sick. Her throat was sore, so she hadn't really been lying. Lauren suspected Linus wouldn't buy her excuse, but that was tough. With a little luck, she had passed her germs along to him. If his throat started to scratch, then he might believe her.

Groaning inwardly, she recalled the party the night before. It was too bad Jerome was dead, but Lauren felt far worse that Yelena had walked in on her and Linus. That wasn't going to help in her quest for Constance's job. As far as Lauren could tell, Yelena was one uptight woman, and Lauren strongly doubted the news president would shrug off the compromising scene. If Yelena wasn't on her side, Lauren could kiss her ambitions at KEY good-bye.

She pulled the sleep mask from her eyes and searched for the remote control. *KEY to America* was just beginning.

Standing on the stage, Constance Young was resplendent in a bright red suit.

"Good morning. Today we come to you from Radio City Music Hall, home of the world-renowned Christmas Spectacular. A cast of one hundred and forty people, including the dazzling Rockettes with their famous eye-high kicks, will be with us this morning, and we'll have a visit from Santa Claus, who has sneaked in from the North Pole, but first we have the morning headlines."

It was so incongruous, thought Lauren, as she studied Constance. The happy banter of the scripted opening leading to the serious news. But they had to get the viewers into the tent, Linus always said, promising them a good time if they could just sit through the nitty-gritty.

"Anthrax has taken the life of thirty-six-year-old KEY News Producer Jerome Henning, a staff member of our broadcast. Henning, who had been in critical condition at a New Jersey hospital, died yesterday. Police found anthrax in Henning's home and are investigating a possible link to anthrax taken from a lab where the former KEY medical correspondent, Dr. John Lee, shot his report on the availability of the deadly substance. In his report, Dr. Lee claimed to have obtained his own container of anthrax, but tests showed that substance to be powdered sugar."

Lauren rose from her bed and went into the bathroom. As she splashed cold water on her face, she mapped out her morning. The first stop was the doctor's office. Before she did anything else, she was going to get that Cipro. If this sore throat was the beginning of anything more serious than a cold, she had to be protected.

CHAPTER 93

The mighty Wurlitzer organ played, more than four thousand pipes filling the gigantic hall with the strains of "Silver Bells." It's Christmastime in the city. Annabelle felt a tear roll down her cheek as she stood at the side of the stage and listened to the sweet music.

Jerome had loved the holiday season so. He'd been like a little kid that Christmas they'd been together, insisting they do the things that make New York so magical at this time of year. Ice skating at Rockefeller Center, touring the aisles full of toys at F.A.O. Schwarz, riding in a horse-drawn carriage through snowy Central Park. He'd told her he hoped they would be together forever as they huddled beneath the carriage robes in the back of the hansom cab.

But when she'd met Mike, she knew that he was the one for her. Even if she hadn't fallen in love with Mike, Annabelle was sure she wouldn't have ended up with Jerome. There were things about Jerome that had made Annabelle hold back. He was smart and creative and loved to have fun, but with Jerome, there had been an undercurrent of danger as well. She was aware that he dabbled with drugs, and Annabelle instinctively knew that, great though their times together were, this was not the person with whom she could envision having children.

Still, as the organ finished the holiday tune, Annabelle mourned the loss of Jerome. His end had come too soon and too horribly. She could not understand why he would have had anthrax in his home. Jerome may have liked to live on the edge, may have used cocaine at one time, but she couldn't believe that he would be playing around with something as dangerous as anthrax.

It didn't make sense.

How had the anthrax gotten there? Had Jerome taken it from Dr. Lee? But why would he have done that? Did he want to poison himself?

Annabelle dismissed the thought of suicide. Jerome had been too excited about the prospects for selling his manuscript. He had been looking forward with high hopes. No, Annabelle was sure Jerome had not intentionally taken his own life. Either he had taken the anthrax for some other unknown reason and inadvertently exposed himself, or someone else had carried anthrax into his home.

The obvious suspect was John Lee. Had Lee planted the anthrax at Jerome's and contaminated Annabelle's office as well? Could he have known about his unflattering portrayal in Jerome's manuscript?

Was that a reason to kill someone?

CHAPTER 94

The persistent banging awakened him from his fitful sleep. He threw back the covers, pulled on a robe, and stumbled, bleary-eyed, to the front door.

"Who is it?"

"FBI. Open up."

Damn. His mind searched frantically for his options. There were none. Resigned, John Lee undid the double locks.

"You have the right to remain silent . . ." began the warning.

"I want to call my lawyer," Lee protested.

"You'll have that chance. But first, you're coming with us."

CHAPTER 95

From the control room, Linus ogled the monitor as the Rockettes strutted their stuff. Dressed as Santa's reindeer, those dames just oozed sex appeal. A little sex in the morning never hurt anyone.

"Get a look at those legs." One of the technicians whistled.

"Camera Two, pan down the dance line," ordered the director.

It was getting near the inevitable. The part that everyone waited for: the famous precision kick line. As the shapely legs rose high, shouts went up in the control room.

"Go, baby. Go."

"Take it home, Momma."

Linus enjoyed the bawdy comments of the workers he made sure were assigned to his control room as he scanned the other monitors to see what the competition was doing. None of them—*Today, Good Morning America, The Early Show*—had anything that was as mesmerizing as this. He smiled with pleasure. This morning's broadcast was damn fine television, up to his exacting standard. It didn't happen by accident. But then, not much worthwhile did.

Inside, *KTA* might be in a state of flux, but the viewers at home sure couldn't see it. They couldn't see the solemn expressions on the staffers' faces or hear the worried whispers. They couldn't know the executive producer was relieved that Jerome Henning could pose no future threat.

Linus's ghostwriter was now truly a ghost.

CHAPTER 96

It had been a deadly weekend.

The metal vaults were filled, and the county morgue was understaffed and overworked. The medical examiner checked his list of bodies destined for the autopsy knife.

Clara Romanski was going to have to wait her turn.

CHAPTER 97

After the show at Radio City, Annabelle took a taxi to the Broadcast Center and found, as expected, her office sealed shut. She wanted to see if she had any messages and used one of the phones at the central news desk to check.

"Hi, Annabelle. This is Peter Henning. Just wanted to let you know that I am flying back to California this morning. The funeral home is taking care of the arrangements for Jerome. His body is being cremated. We're not having a formal funeral. Jerome never liked them. Maybe we'll arrange a memorial sometime later."

Peter recited his home phone number. Annabelle jotted it down.

"You look pale, Annabelle. Are you feeling all right?" Still wearing her coat, Beth had come into the newsroom.

"That was Jerome's brother. Jerome is being cremated, and there won't be a funeral," Annabelle said softly.

If she had expected Beth to share her upset, Annabelle was disappointed.

"That doesn't surprise me or distress me," Beth replied, her voice flat. "Jerome shouldn't have a church funeral. It would be hypocritical."

"Oh, Beth. How can you say that?" Annabelle asked with dismay.

"Easy. Jerome didn't respect the sanctity of human life." Beth turned and walked away, leaving Annabelle slack-jawed.

The second message was from Yelena Gregory's office. Annabelle called the extension and was told by Yelena's secretary to report to the news president's office as soon as possible. The two FBI agents who had questioned her last week were with Yelena when she arrived.

As Annabelle took a seat, Yelena gave her the headlines. "Dr. Lee has been taken into custody, Annabelle, as has the laboratory employee who admitted to helping smuggle out the anthrax."

"We're trying to figure out the connection between Dr. Lee and the anthrax found in Jerome Henning's home, Ms. Murphy," began Agent Lyons. "We're hoping you might be able to help us with that."

Annabelle waited for a question. She felt heat rising to her face and wondered if the agents noticed it. Would it make her look guilty of something?

"Do you know of any reason why Mr. Henning would have had the anthrax?"

"No."

"Do you know of any reason Mr. Henning would have wanted to obtain anthrax as a weapon?"

"Certainly not."

"Would Mr. Henning have wanted Dr. Lee to look stupid? Would he have wanted to embarrass Dr. Lee for any reason?"

"I don't understand what you mean."

Agent Lyons looked squarely at Annabelle. "Well, Dr. Lee was certainly humiliated when the container he claimed on national television to be anthrax turned out to be sugar. Could Mr. Henning have switched the test tubes in order to make Dr. Lee look foolish?"

Annabelle answered with conviction. "Look, Jerome didn't care for Dr. Lee. That's no secret. But I can't believe he would have gone to such lengths, taken such a risk, just to make Lee look like an ass."

Without expression, Agent Lyons flipped through her notes. "Joe Connelly tells us that you had a copy of a manuscript Mr. Henning had been working on. One that depicted members of the *KTA* staff in a less-than-flattering light."

Annabelle glanced at Yelena. The reputation of KEY News was everything to her. Annabelle shuddered to think what Yelena would do if she read Jerome's manuscript.

"Yes, that's right," she answered.

"And that manuscript was stolen from you on Friday night?"

"Yes."

"But you didn't report that to the police."

"I didn't think it was important, at first," Annabelle explained. "I've had my purse stolen before. I know from experience that it's not a police priority to track down a petty thief. It wasn't until later that it occurred to me the target might have been the manuscript rather than my tote bag. As soon as I realized this, I called Joe. He told me he would let the appropriate authorities know."

The FBI agent nodded. "Yes. Mr. Connelly informed us, and we understand you were going to write down what you remembered of the manuscript."

"I have, in longhand. I can type it up for you as soon as I leave here." Annabelle was aching to get out of this stifling room. But the agents weren't done with her yet. The male agent took up the questioning now.

"Leo McGillicuddy, Ms. Murphy." He identified himself for her again. "Can you think of any reason why someone would want to poison Jerome Henning and then plant the anthrax at his home?"

Annabelle considered her response. "I suppose there were reasons in that manuscript of his, if someone was desperate enough not to want to see an unflattering portrayal of him- or herself published. That's why I think I should go type up my notes for you."

She started to rise from her chair.

"Wait a minute, Ms. Murphy. We're not through here yet."

Annabelle sat back down.

"We're curious. Why do you think there were anthrax spores found in your office?"

Oh my God. They're looking at me as a suspect. Annabelle's heart raced.

"I think I should get an attorney."

"Do you have something to hide?"

"No. But I think *you* may think I do."

CHAPTER 98

Annabelle wasn't taking this seriously enough.

Wearing the rubber gloves he'd found under the kitchen sink, Mike searched through the bedroom closet, trying to remember what Annabelle had worn to work last week. She would be furious that he was throwing out that cashmere sweater he'd given her, but he'd buy her a new one for Christmas. He threw the yellow sweater into a large black plastic garbage bag, along with her black slacks and the gray suit he thought she'd worn on Friday. Two pairs of black leather shoes went into the bag as well. He tied the bag up tight.

As he reached the front door, he thought of something else. That navy wool coat. Annabelle had been complaining that it was worn out anyway. Might as well get rid of it too. Mike took it from the foyer closet and stuffed it into the reopened bag.

He felt a sense of satisfaction as he took the elevator down without his usual panic of late. He really was getting better. Mike whistled as he walked the few blocks it took to find a Dumpster.

CHAPTER 99

Where was he?

Annabelle listened as the answering machine picked up in their apartment. She hesitated a moment and then hung up without leaving a message. It was probably better not to worry Mike with this right now, leaving him at home, alone, stewing about it all day. She could ask Constance if she knew of a lawyer to contact.

Annabelle gathered the canvas knapsack she had commandeered from the kids' room to use until she got around to buying a new tote bag and headed out of the newsroom. *You have nothing to hide. It will be all right,* she reassured herself as she walked toward Constance's office. *Just keep on telling the truth.*

The door was open, but there was no one inside. Annabelle sat down at the desk, knowing Constance wouldn't mind if she used the computer while she waited. She took out her notes on Jerome's manuscript and began to type. She was almost through her assignment when she felt the hand on her shoulder.

"Oh." She jumped. "You scared me."

Russ Parrish stood too close, his eyes sweeping the computer screen. Hastily, Annabelle clicked a button, and the document faded from view.

"I didn't mean to scare you, Annabelle," he apologized. "I just saw you in here and wanted to tell you how sorry I am about Jerome."

Annabelle nodded, trying to regain her composure. "Thanks, Russ. I know you and he had some good times together too."

"That's right. We sure did. But that was a while ago. We hadn't partied in a long time."

Annabelle waited to see if Russ would explain further.

"You know. People grow apart."

"I guess that's inevitable," she offered.

"Yeah, but I was bummed when it happened with Jerome. He got real serious all of a sudden and cut me off."

Was "getting real serious all of a sudden" code for the fact that Jerome had stopped using cocaine when Russ hadn't? Or had Jerome, when he decided to expose Russ in his book, separated himself from his party companion? Most of all, Annabelle wondered if Russ had just been able to read his damaging portrayal on the computer screen.

"I'm sorry, Russ," she responded, feeling uncomfortable.

"Me too, Annabelle. Me too."

CHAPTER 100

Wayne read the message on the computer screen.

FROM: YELENA GREGORY

TO: ALL PERSONNEL

OUR KEY NEWS COLLEAGUE JEROME HENNING PASSED AWAY YESTERDAY AFTERNOON. JEROME, A MEMBER OF THE KEY NEWS FAMILY FOR TEN YEARS,

WAS A TALENTED PRODUCER, WRITER, AND RESEARCHER WHO BROUGHT CREATIVITY AND CONSIDERABLE ENERGY TO EVERY ASSIGNMENT. HIS BOOK SEGMENTS ON *KEY TO AMERICA* ATTRACTED THE ATTENTION OF MILLIONS OF VIEWERS AND INFLUENCED THE READING HABITS OF PEOPLE IN ALL WALKS OF LIFE.

A MEMORIAL SERVICE FOR JEROME HAS NOT YET BEEN PLANNED, BUT YOU WILL BE INFORMED AS SOON AS ONE IS SCHEDULED.

PLEASE JOIN ME IN EXTENDING OUR SINCERE CONDOLENCES TO THE FAMILY AND FRIENDS OF JEROME HENNING.

Wayne shook his head and sighed.

That's what you got after a decade. Three measly paragraphs, only one that was actually about you. You could work long hours, skip days off and miss vacations, put your mind and soul into your work, take to heart every critical comment that a boss or coworker hurled your way and spend nights tossing and turning as a result. At the end of all that, a Yelena Gregory e-mail was what you got.

And life went right on without you around this place.

Reading the e-mail over again, Wayne noticed Yelena's reference to Jerome's researching skills. That was certainly true enough. The guy knew how to get information, leaving no stone unturned in finding out things that were really none of his business.

Wayne still smarted from the knowledge that Jerome had dug into the local newspaper accounts of Seth's accident all those years ago. One day, Wayne had spotted copies of the old clippings on Jerome's desk.

Jerome should not have been digging into the painful past.

CHAPTER 101

The ladies' room stall was a private place to have a good cry.

God, forgive me. She shouldn't have said what she had to Annabelle. Jerome may have gotten what was coming to him, but it wasn't Christian of her to malign him as she had. It was wrong to curse the dead.

Beth pulled at the roll of toilet paper and wadded the white tissue to wipe her nose and dry her eyes. She came out of the stall and went to the sink. As she pumped liquid soap from the wall dispenser, she stopped.

The stainless steel shelf over the sinks was dusted with white powder.

Joe took the hysterical phone call, ordered the rest room closed, and called the NYPD. The specially trained "hammer team" would be there right away.

Next, he called Yelena.

"God, what else?" she moaned. "We're going to have some panic here. The way news travels around this place, we're going to have a stampede out of the building."

"Not if *we* don't panic, Yelena," Joe answered evenly. "Let's let the professionals come in and see what's what."

Beth lost no time running to the *KTA* newsroom and announcing there could be anthrax in the ladies' room. Though a few workers barely raised their heads from their computer screens, most dropped what they were doing, and three people screamed.

Linus Nazareth poked his head out of his adjoining office to see what the commotion was about.

"There's white powder all over the ladies' room," Beth said breathlessly.

"Did you call Security?"

"Yes."

"Good." Linus turned to address the room. "Now, everyone, let's not panic. I'm going to call Yelena Gregory, and I'll let you know what's going on. In the meantime, just continue doing what you were doing," he commanded, staring pointedly at the people who were going to get their coats.

"You've got to put out some sort of official word, Yelena, fast. Otherwise, we are going to have a mutiny on our hands." Linus held the phone to his ear and stared out his window at the emptying newsroom.

FROM: YELENA GREGORY
TO: ALL PERSONNEL

AN UNKNOWN WHITE POWDER WAS FOUND IN THE *KEY TO AMERICA* LADIES' ROOM THIS MORNING. POLICE AND HEALTH DEPARTMENT OFFICIALS HAVE RESPONDED TO THE SCENE. THE SUBSTANCE IS BEING TESTED, BUT OFFICIALS SUSPECT THAT THE POWDER IS DUST FROM LOOSE BATHROOM-TILE GROUTING.

CHAPTER

102

The nurse entered the vital signs readings on the patient's chart. The middle-aged woman who'd wrapped her car around a telephone pole yesterday still hadn't regained consciousness. But if she had to bet, the nurse would wager that Evelyn Wilkie was going to come through, in her own time.

She patted the cotton blanket that covered the still body and vowed to herself to be very careful on her own ride home later. That ice was treacherous.

CHAPTER 103

After handing over her manuscript outline, Annabelle phoned and got the welcome confirmation. Her nasal swab had come back negative. Constance's lawyer friend had agreed to represent her if need be. All in all, a productive, if hectic and uneasy, morning.

She called home again, this time to share the negative test results with Mike. As the phone rang, unanswered, Annabelle felt the worry that had become her familiar companion. Where was he? What was he doing? Was Mike all right?

There was nothing she could do right now, she told herself, except try to think positively. She would call again later and just pray that Mike would be there for the kids after school. She had to try to let herself trust him again, know that he would act responsibly.

Realizing she hadn't had anything to eat except the half a bagel she had wolfed down in the cab on the way to Radio City, Annabelle grabbed her wallet and headed toward the cafeteria. She scanned the salad bar and grill station but decided on a BLT on whole wheat from the deli.

Getting in the checkout line, she thought of poor Edgar and his family. This would be such a sad holiday for them. This Thanksgiving and the ones to come would be marked with the memory of his death.

The cashier rang up the sandwich and the diet Coke.

"May, do you know any of the details about Edgar's funeral?" Annabelle asked.

The heavyset woman nodded solemnly. "It's tomorrow night at the Calvary Baptist Church in the Bronx. Seven o'clock."

Annabelle thanked the cashier, considering it strange that a funeral would he held in the evening, but thinking it might work out for her to attend. So much of everyone's focus had been on Jerome. Edgar's life wasn't any less important.

CHAPTER 104

Lily was relieved to hear that Gavin Winston had called in sick. She had been dreading coming in to work all weekend. She had almost called in herself to say that she wasn't feeling well, but she wanted to have a perfect attendance record for her internship.

She had talked with her roommate about the uncomfortable situation, showing her friend a copy of Winston's e-mail. Her friend was enraged at what she thought to be blatant sexual harassment and urged that Lily complain to the higher-ups.

There was no one higher than Yelena Gregory.

Lily gathered up her courage and walked down to the president's office. The secretary was checking the calendar for an appointment time when Yelena came out of her office and looked at Lily with interest.

"Yelena Gregory." She extended her hand.

"Yes, I know." The younger woman was flustered. "I'm Lily Dalton. I'm interning at *KTA*."

"Nice to meet you, Lily."

"I was wondering if I could speak to you for a minute."

Yelena looked at her watch. "All right, but that's just about all the time I have. Come in."

The moment the intern left the office, Yelena picked up the phone and called Information Services.

"I want a blind cc put on all Gavin Winston's e-mails," she ordered. "And call up the e-mails of the past year."

"No problem, Ms. Gregory," came the response. "We know the routine."

CHAPTER 105

Gavin exited Saks Fifth Avenue and walked the several blocks north, cursing Marguerite for the substantial charges he had been forced to make to his credit card. The giant electronic snowflake hung, already lit, high above the intersection of

Fifty-seventh Street, announcing to the well-heeled consumers pounding the sidewalks that the Christmas consumption season had begun.

He wore his newly purchased pin-striped suit, having shipped the one he'd been wearing for days to his home in Connecticut, since he didn't want to carry it with him. Gavin realized now that that could have been a mistake. If Marguerite took in the package, she would have a fit when she opened it, crazed that it might be contaminated. Perhaps she'd even throw it out. The thought of that made his stomach tighten. That was one of his favorite suits, bought on his last trip to London.

As he turned west on Fifty-seventh, Gavin looked at his reflection in the plate-glass windows. A tall, distinguished-looking, gray-haired man striding purposefully toward his destination. Not a sniveling, henpecked husband!

He was going home tonight, whether Marguerite wanted him to or not. But first he had to get into the office and check his e-mail to see if dinner was on with Lily, and he wanted to see if there were any new developments with Wellstone and the SEC investigation. If anyone asked, he was going to say he still didn't feel well but he had some things that just couldn't wait, the implication being that he was devoted to the job, no matter what.

He wasn't concerned about anthrax exposure anymore. He had started his Cipro.

CHAPTER

106

Yelena crafted the message herself, hoping the news would help allay the fears in the Broadcast Center.

FROM: YELENA GREGORY
TO: ALL PERSONNEL

THE NASAL SWAB RESULTS ARE BACK AND, I AM DELIGHTED TO REPORT, NOT A SINGLE CASE OF ANTHRAX EXPOSURE HAS BEEN FOUND. WITH THIS HAPPY NEWS, I HOPE THAT EACH AND EVERY ONE OF YOU WILL BREATHE EASIER. AUTHORITIES ARE CONTINUING TO INVESTIGATE THE DEATHS OF OUR COLLEAGUE JEROME HENNING AND FOOD-SERVICE WORKER EDGAR RIVERS. WE HAVE EVERY CONFIDENCE THAT THE POLICE AND FBI ARE USING THEIR CONSIDERABLE RESOURCES TO SOLVE THESE CASES, AND KEY NEWS WILL CONTINUE TO COOPERATE TOWARD THAT END.

DR. JOHN LEE, FORMER KEY NEWS CORRESPONDENT, HAS BEEN TAKEN INTO CUSTODY

FOR HIS ALLEGED CONNECTION TO THE ANTHRAX THAT KILLED JEROME HENNING.

MEANTIME, PLEASE LET ME THANK ALL OF YOU FOR THE PROFESSIONALISM YOU SHOW EACH AND EVERY DAY, AND PARTICULARLY AT THIS DIFFICULT TIME. KEY NEWS REMAINS THE LEADER IN THE BROADCAST NEWS FIELD BECAUSE OF THE INTEGRITY AND TALENT OF ALL OF YOU.

KEEP UP THE GREAT WORK DURING THIS DIFFICULT TIME.

CHAPTER 107

Lauren came home from the pharmacy and, with resolve, swallowed the first of the pills. She switched on the television and caught the rest of *Oprah,* marveling as always at how a young black woman, with no connections to speak of, had managed to build a multimillion-dollar communications empire. If Oprah could do it, so could she, or at least come pretty damn close.

Inspired, Lauren rose from the sofa, went to her desk, and tapped at the computer keys, signing on to collect her e-mails at home.

As she read Yelena's message, she wondered if she should have bothered with the Cipro. But experience had shown her that the corporate line wasn't always the whole truth. Sometimes management would say whatever was necessary to further its own agenda. Yelena would naturally want to reassure the staff so they would keep on working.

Lauren decided she was glad she had gone ahead and started the powerful antibiotic. She was determined to survive this mess at KEY. Survive and come out on top.

CHAPTER 108

The anthrax-laced tissue hadn't found its intended mark.

Annabelle Murphy was walking around the Broadcast Center healthy as could be.

With her knowledge of what was in Henning's manuscript and her ability to re-create her own version of it if she wanted to, Annabelle was an unacceptable threat.

There was too much at stake here.

The decision had already been made to eliminate Annabelle. If the anthrax hadn't worked, another, more immediate method would have to be found.

CHAPTER 109

Annabelle was exhausted. She'd been up since 4:00 A.M., after getting to bed late the night before. The afternoon had been spent getting her part of things finalized for the Tuesday morning show at the Statue of Liberty and Ellis Island. Constance and Harry had provided the old photographs of their ancestors, who had been among the 12 million immigrants who approached America's "front doors to freedom," searching for personal liberties and dreaming of economic opportunity in the United States.

The producer's job was to fashion two, ninety-second packages, explaining the ethnic background of each of the

KTA hosts, the history of their families, and their pursuit of the American dream. As Annabelle searched the Ellis Island Web site for material, she vowed to ask her mother about their family. It would be nice at some point, if she ever had the time, to put together something like this for her own children about their family's roots in America.

She wrote up the scripts, faxed copies to Constance and Harry at home, and took in their narrations over the phone line. She left the recorded tracks and the video of the still pictures along with some very old newsreel footage taken in the great, echoing Registry Room at Ellis Island, which Wayne had dug up for her with one of *KTA*'s best videotape editors. Leaving everything in expert hands, Annabelle could go home with confidence. She wanted to get down-town as soon as she could. Though Mike had sounded fine when she finally reached him to tell him that her anthrax test had come back negative, what if it all became too much for him?

By instinct, she headed to her office before remembering that it was still sealed shut. She turned in the direction of Constance's room, where she had parked her jacket and other belongings. Wayne Nazareth met her in the hall. He looked pale.

"That file video you found is great, Wayne," she greeted him. "Thanks a lot."

"Good. I hope it helps," he answered. "You going home now?"

"Yes. I have to be out on Ellis Island very early in the morning."

"Me, too. See you there, Annabelle."

Annabelle's eyes followed him as he walked, hunch-shouldered, down the hallway.

Annabelle popped her head into Beth Terry's office on her way out of the building. The unit manager was eating a large slab of chocolate cake. *So much for that diet of hers.*

"Okay, Beth. I'll see you in the morning. I'm going home."

"I'm almost finished here too," Beth responded, hastily wiping her mouth with a napkin, looking a bit embarrassed. "I just have to check that the remote lines are all ordered."

"Good. I'll be in at five." Annabelle turned to go.

"Annabelle?"

"Yes?"

"I'm sorry about what I said to you before about Jerome. That wasn't right of me. I know you cared about him, and I know he cared about you. Very much."

"That's all right, Beth." Annabelle was tempted to say more, to see if the woman wanted to talk about her own relationship with Jerome. But Beth bent her head down, intent on the cake on the paper plate.

She had the strangest feeling as she walked toward the subway at Columbus Circle, as if she were being followed. But each time Annabelle turned to look behind her, the people on the sidewalk were different and none of the faces was recognizable.

She waited on the platform for just a few minutes before the Number 1 train lumbered into the station. Annabelle stepped onboard along with the hordes of rush-hour riders. The rhythmic clatter of the subway car on the metal tracks lulled her as it traveled beneath the city streets. She mustn't fall asleep. She didn't want to miss her stop.

Annabelle got off at Christopher Street and climbed the stairs to street level. The cold night air felt bracing and good.

She stopped at their favorite Thai restaurant and ordered some chicken satays with extra peanut sauce for the twins and two orders of num-tok beef because she and Mike loved the hot chilies and lime. Takeout again, but the kids would be thrilled. She was just too tired to think about cooking tonight.

As Annabelle left the restaurant, she felt glad that they lived in Greenwich Village, where everything was so convenient. All they needed was in walking distance of their apartment. Grocery, newsstand, dry cleaner, drugstore—and every kind of eatery imaginable. She was waiting with all the others returning home at the end of the workday for the light to turn at the corner, lost in her reverie, when the strong arms came from behind, pushing her into the path of an oncoming bus.

The sound of screeching brakes sliced through the night air.

"Oh my God," screamed an elderly woman on the side-walk.

Annabelle felt herself tumbling forward, sliding toward the bus. There was absolutely nothing she could do. *The kids. Mike.*

It happened in just a few seconds, but there was an excruciating slowness to it all. It was coming at her. What would it feel like?

In that last moment, Annabelle realized she might have a chance if she fell to the ground and rolled under the body of the bus, between the wheels. The bus might go right over her.

She aimed and dove to the macadam, closing her eyes,

waiting for the impact of the giant steel vehicle. When she opened her eyes again, she was staring up at a dark mass of pipes and fittings, the underbelly of the bus.

The crowd gathered quickly.

"Are you all right, lady?" asked the ashen-faced bus driver, squatting down to peer at her.

"Yes. I think so."

Slowly, Annabelle slid, caterpillarlike, from beneath the bus. The driver reached out to her, helping her rise to her feet. Annabelle could feel his hand shaking, or was it her own?

"Thank God, you're all right," he whispered.

In the bus lights, Annabelle caught sight of the steaming chicken satays strewn over the road. She began to take stock. Her slacks were torn, and she could feel that her knee was cut. The palms of her hands were scraped raw. But, miraculously, nothing else seemed to be damaged.

Someone returned her purse and knapsack. Another Good Samaritan insisted on walking her the rest of the way home, very, very slowly.

Huddled in a storefront doorway, the attacker watched as the crowd dispersed.

CHAPTER

110

It was grilled-cheese sandwiches and Campbell's tomato soup for dinner that night. Mike did the cooking while Annabelle lay on the sofa. He brought her a mug of hot soup and a couple of Tylenol.

"Take these," he urged. "I never thought I'd say this, but let's leave this city. I hate it here. Let's go somewhere nice and quiet, where planes don't fly into buildings and people don't get pushed under buses."

She swallowed the tablets obediently, chased them with the creamy soup. The warm liquid felt good going down. The thought of living in a peaceful little town was very attractive right now.

"I don't understand why the police weren't called, Annabelle," Mike pressed.

"There really wasn't any need to, Mike. I was all right."

"But you think someone pushed you in front of that bus." He was looking at her incredulously.

"I don't know," said Annabelle, pausing to take another

sip of soup. "The more I think about it, maybe I was just jostled by the crowd. I can't be sure that someone pushed me."

"And you can't be sure you weren't," Mike insisted. "With all that's been happening around you, I think you have to call the police and report this. If you don't, I will."

"All right. I will. I will."

"Good." He handed her the cordless phone. "You do that, and I'll give the kids their baths."

"Daddy, look." Thomas held out his hand.

Mike wiped away the soap suds. "What, Thomas? I don't see anything."

"Next to my boo-boo, Daddy. There's a bump next to it."

His father bent down close to inspect the small finger. "It looks like the cut is healing fine, Thomas."

"But it itches me," the boy whined.

"Honey, maybe you've got a little bug bite there, but it's nothing to worry about. Now, come on, let's get you dried off and into your pajamas."

TUESDAY

NOVEMBER 25

CHAPTER

111

"What? Are you trying to win a medal for Martyr of the Year?" Mike had turned on the light and was sitting up in bed watching her get dressed.

Annabelle uttered a heavy sigh. "Don't give me any grief, Mike. I'm not in the mood."

Now that was a role reversal. These last months it had been Mike doing the snapping at her. It felt liberating to let loose with her own exasperation for a change.

Her body ached, and she winced as she pulled her panty hose over the bandage on her knee. It suddenly occurred to her that it was going to be freezing out there in the harbor today. She pulled off the stockings and rummaged through the dresser, looking for a pair of thermal leggings to wear under her slacks.

"Annabelle. It's all right to take a day off once in a while. You slid under a bus last night, for God's sake. If Linus Nazareth doesn't understand that, then you should be looking for another boss." There was anger in his voice.

She spun to face her husband. "Linus Nazareth wouldn't care if I'd been *hit* by the bus. All he cares about is his show. And as for looking for another boss, if you hadn't noticed, Mike, jobs are hard to come by right now. It's brutal out there, and this family needs my job to survive."

Annabelle regretted her words the minute she stopped speaking. The wounded expression on Mike's face wasn't worth her momentary release.

"I'm sorry, honey," she whispered, going to the bed and sitting down beside him.

"No, you're right. I haven't been holding up my end of things," Mike said quietly. "I've let you and the kids down."

"Oh, Mike, please don't feel like that. You've been through so much, sweetheart. Because you're such a dear and decent person, your system just couldn't take it. And, you know, honey, you're not the only one that's reacted this way. Lots of people are in the same boat."

Mike bit his lower lip and stared down at his hands. "But I am feeling better, Annabelle. Maybe I'll be able to go back to the job soon."

With tenderness, Annabelle kissed him on the cheek. "I know you will, Mike, when you're ready. And if you decide that you want to change careers, leave the fire department, leave New York City, that will be fine too. I'll support you in whatever you want to do. But, in the meantime, we have to pay our bills. Let me go do my job."

Annabelle uttered an oath as she searched the closet.

"What's wrong?" Mike asked.

"I can't find my black wool slacks."

"They aren't there, Annabelle." He had forgotten to tell her.

"Oh, did you drop them off at the cleaners?"

"No," he defied her. "I threw them out."

She looked at him in puzzlement.

"I threw out the things you wore last week."

"You're kidding, right?"

"No, I'm not kidding. I wasn't going to take any chances with anthrax."

Annabelle had neither the time nor the inclination to get into another argument with him. Exasperated, she turned back to the closet and picked out something else to wear.

CHAPTER

112

It was a cold, dark ferry ride to Ellis Island. Whipped by the damp wind, Annabelle started by standing alone on the deck outside, contemplating Lady Liberty in the quiet harbor. But after a few minutes she moved inside to watch from behind the windows. It was going to be a long day, and she knew she should conserve her energy.

The plan was for Harry Granger to report from the Statue of Liberty while Constance would be stationed at the Ellis Island Immigration Museum. Annabelle was relieved to see that Constance was already on the boat. She took a seat beside her friend, holding out her scraped palms and explaining what had happened on the way home from work the evening before.

"Mike insisted that I call the police, though I'm not even sure I was actually pushed."

"Well, Mike was right." Constance was adamant. "What did the police say?"

"They took down the information, but I didn't get the

impression there was anything much they could really do about it. I didn't have a description to give them, and any eyewitnesses at the scene were long since gone. Unless somebody comes forward and says that he or she saw someone push me, the cops really don't have anything to go on."

The ferry let them off at the entrance to the island. As Annabelle approached the majestic Main Building, with its tiles and turrets and copper domes, she tried to imagine what it must have been like to be an immigrant here. To arrive at this place after a long ocean voyage, carrying everything you had in a battered satchel, unable to speak the language of the new country. What complex and conflicting emotions there must have been. Leaving your homeland and the people you loved behind while looking forward to a better life in an unfamiliar America.

Annabelle and Constance entered the Baggage Room, the point where the immigrants first set foot into the Main Building. Beth Terry was waiting amid the period baggage displayed around the room.

"You'll probably want to take a walk around," she suggested, handing Constance a packet of information, "and familiarize yourself with the place."

"What do you need me to do?" asked Annabelle.

"We're in good shape right now. But when the guests arrive, you'll be in charge of escorting them."

"Fine. That's easy enough. In the meantime, I'll keep Constance company. I've never been here myself, and I've been looking forward to seeing this place." It was one of the great things about her job, being exposed to things she might not have been otherwise, while getting paid.

They walked through the now magnificently restored Registry Room, once the focal point of the immigrants' processing, the place where newcomers underwent questioning and were either given permission to stay or denied entry into the United States. They gazed at the Wall of Honor, with 420,000 immigrant entries, the largest wall of names in the world. They couldn't cover the thirty galleries and exhibits that Constance's notes indicated were filled with artifacts, historic photos and posters, oral histories, and ethnic music, all telling the story of what happened at Ellis Island and to the newcomers who helped settle America. But they did make sure to look at the Hearing Room, a small courtroom of sorts where disputed cases were decided. The last stop was the Bunk Area, where many immigrants spent the night.

"Can you imagine being stacked up like that, Annabelle?"

"Horrible." She shuddered. "But if you're desperate enough, you can put up with a lot," Annabelle answered.

"What's wrong?" Constance asked, observing the pained expression on her friend's face.

"It's just my knee. I think I better go back and try to sit down for a while before the show." As she walked away, gingerly putting pressure on her sore leg, Annabelle thought about how close she had come to catastrophe. If she had been killed, could Mike have raised the kids alone? Could he handle that?

For his entertainment segment, Russ had put together a montage of clips from movies about the immigrant experience. He had included *The Immigrant,* Charlie Chaplin's chronicle of his own immigration to America in 1910; Elia Kazan's *America, America,* presenting the dream of coming to America for nineteenth-century immigrants; Coppola's *Godfather, Part II,* the sequel that contrasted the life of the don with the early days of his father as an immigrant to New York City; and *Far and Away,* a Ron Howard film about an Irish tenant farmer who meets the daughter of a wealthy landowner and sets sail for America and the 1893 Oklahoma land rush.

Instead of having Dominick O'Donnell screen it, as the senior producer normally would, Linus insisted on seeing the piece himself before it aired. Russ didn't like the scrutiny one bit.

He waited tensely as the video and narration played on

the monitor and was relieved when Linus announced his verdict: "Nice piece."

Before Russ could say "thanks," Linus had turned and walked away.

He shouldn't have worried. There was no editorial content to this piece, no reviewing done or judgments passed. It was a straight overview, done in workmanlike fashion. Just the facts, ma'am.

But the clips were all of movies made in the past. Nothing soon to be released. Nothing that, by touting it to the public, could earn Russ any money. Until things quieted down a bit at *KTA*, Russ was going to lay low, play it safe, and give Linus exactly what he wanted.

Annabelle escorted the guest and his paraphernalia through the Baggage Room.

"You can set up right here," she indicated.

As the representative of the luggage company arranged modern suitcases in an array of shapes, sizes, and colors, Lauren Adams arrived.

"We'll start off with showing the viewer some of the sacks and duffels that the immigrants used and compare them with what's available to consumers today." Lauren reviewed the aim of the segment for the luggage rep's benefit.

Annabelle consulted her clipboard to see who was arriving next and began to walk back to the entrance of the Main Building.

"Annabelle, you're limping," Lauren called. "What happened?"

"I fell. It's no big deal. I'll be fine."

Lauren looked after her with skepticism.

He spotted her at the refreshment table and walked over and poured himself a cup of coffee.

"I looked for you when I came into the office yesterday afternoon, Lily. I had hoped that we were going to have our dinner together," Gavin purred. *Instead, after I finished what I had to do, I went home to Marguerite,* he seethed inwardly.

"I'm sorry, Mr. Winston. I couldn't make it," said the intern, grabbing her donut. "I've got to go. I promised Beth I would help her with something."

Watching her hasty retreat, Gavin knew. Lily was avoiding him. There was no doubt about it.

He had seen this sort of thing happen before, too many times.

With a wireless microphone clipped to the collar of her sweater, Constance walked through the cavernous Registry Room and recited the words of Emma Lazarus written in 1883.

"Give me your tired, your poor, your huddled masses yearning to breathe free, the wretched refuse of your teeming shore. Send these, the homeless, tempest-tost to me, I lift my lamp beside the golden door."

Aerial pictures of the Statue of Liberty and Ellis Island were beamed from the helicopter flying above to viewers in homes across America.

"Good morning, I'm Constance Young, reporting this morning from the Ellis Island Immigration Museum."

In the control room back at the Broadcast Center, the command was given, switching the cameras.

"And I'm Harry Granger at the Statue of Liberty." Harry appeared, red-nosed, at the base of the statue. "It's Tuesday, November twenty-fifth, and this is *KEY to America.*"

Constance was up again.

"During its peak years, Ellis Island received thousands of immigrants a day. Each hopeful human being was inspected for disability or disease as the long line of new arrivals made their way up the steep stairs to this great room. Over one hundred million Americans can trace their ancestry in the United States to a man, woman, or child whose name was registered here in an inspector's record book. For those immigrants, this spot was *their* 'key to America'."

Nice tie-in, thought Annabelle as she listened and watched from the back of the giant room, just before she heard shouting from outside.

Annabelle slipped out of the great hall, following the noise.

"What's going on?" she called to the technicians who were scurrying away from what she remembered to be the room where the immigrant cases were decided, the Hearing Room.

"Somebody spotted white powder on the floor in there."

The room was sealed off, the police summoned, and the plans scuttled for the segment to be shot in the Hearing Room, all without the viewers at home suspecting anything was amiss. The *KTA* staffers continued with their jobs, glancing furtively at their watches, counting the minutes until the broadcast would be over and they could get back on the ferry.

By the end of the show, the police were fairly sure that the white powder was merely donut sugar, unwittingly sprinkled by a broadcasting snacker.

CHAPTER 113

This was no way to live.

Annabelle felt the anger rise within her as she and the others took the ferry back across the water. The majestic Statue of Liberty held her torch into the overcast morning sky, the symbol of freedom. The copper-skinned lady with her flowing robe and sandaled feet stood tall and proud and strong in the harbor, while Annabelle's coworkers, American citizens, riding on the ferry with her now, were skittish and uncertain.

Damn this new world of unknowable, unexpected terrorism and events too horrible to wrap your mind around. People should not have to live this way, worried about what fresh hell awaited them as they went about their daily routines.

In frustration, Annabelle banged her hand against the railing, wincing as her scraped palm hit the metal, reminding her of the accident the night before. If it was an accident.

As she got off the boat, Annabelle was resolute. Though

she might not be able to control the state of global politics or the intentions of terrorists, she was determined to do what she could to find out who had brought anthrax and fear into her life.

CHAPTER 114

Clara Romanski was first on the list this morning.

The body was pulled from the long drawer and wheeled under the bright lights, and the autopsy began.

"Markedly enlarged hemorrhagic mediastinal lymph nodes on gross examination," the masked man noted out loud.

The medical examiner carved out samples of the spleen and liver to send to the lab for further tests.

CHAPTER

115

Feeling that she should reassure the staff about the frenzy over the white powder at Ellis Island, Yelena arrived at the morning meeting.

"The test has already confirmed what the police suspected. The powder was merely donut sugar," she announced.

"They're sure it wasn't anthrax?" Wayne asked anxiously. "I was in that room."

"Yes. They're sure. So none of you have anything to worry about."

"For now," Gavin muttered under his breath.

Yelena shot him a withering stare. "That kind of cynical attitude doesn't get us anywhere, Gavin." He should only know that she was getting her file together on him. Another incriminating e-mail or two and he would be out.

"If there aren't any other questions, go on with your meeting," Yelena directed.

"We're going to have a real nor'easter blowing in overnight," Caridad Vega announced.

"How long will it last?" asked Linus, the next morning's show his only concern.

The weather forecaster shrugged. "It could go into tomorrow afternoon."

The plans for doing the broadcast outside, in front of the department store Christmas windows, were scrubbed.

"Okay. We're in the studio tomorrow. We'll do the windows on Friday instead," Linus decided.

"I'm all for that," remarked Harry Granger. "After freezing my buns off out with Lady Liberty this morning, the nice, warm studio suits me just fine."

The change required a total overhaul of the broadcast, and the meeting ran long as the new assignments were given out.

"All right, everybody. That's it. Go to it," Linus commanded.

"Wait a minute. I have something I want to say."

Linus looked at Annabelle as if she had two heads. A meeting was over when he said it was. No one else called the shots.

Annabelle could tell her boss was annoyed, but she plowed ahead anyway. "Look, I feel I have earned the right to say these things," she began. "I've lost a good friend, and something of his which he entrusted to me has been stolen from me. Anthrax has been detected in my office, and last night, on the way home from work, someone may have tried to push me in front of a bus."

The group assembled around the conference table murmured.

"So that's why you're limping?" Lauren interjected, pleased with her observation.

"Yes, that's why I'm limping, and that's why my hands look like this." Annabelle held up her palms for the gaping group to see.

"Oh, Annabelle, that's terrible," cried Beth.

"Look, I'll be fine," Annabelle said, brushing the sympathy away. "But now it occurs to me that though Dr. Lee is in custody for his anthrax stunt and it might even turn out that he somehow contaminated Jerome, he certainly wasn't in Greenwich Village last evening when that bus came my way. And if someone is trying to get rid of me, I need to figure out who it is."

"Have you notified the police about the bus accident, Annabelle?" Yelena asked.

"Yes."

"Then they'll be working on it."

"With all due respect, Yelena, I don't think that's good enough. By the time the police figure things out, if they even do, it could be too late. Look at Edgar Rivers. Have they gotten anywhere with that?"

Yelena's silence was the answer.

"So here's what I'm asking," Annabelle implored. "If any of you have any ideas or know anything that you think might help in figuring out what's been happening around here, I want you to come and talk to me about it. Or better yet, I'll be coming around to talk to all of you."

"Annabelle, that's the job of the police," Yelena insisted.

"I'm sorry, Yelena, but I am a firm believer in taking my destiny in my own hands. Scraped though they may be."

CHAPTER 116

Evelyn blinked her eyes open, aware of the pounding in her head.

Where was she?

A woman dressed in white stood beside her bed.

"Good morning, Mrs. Wilkie. Welcome back," said the nurse in a soothing voice.

"What happened?" Evelyn whispered, trying to recall.

"You had an accident, Mrs. Wilkie, and you've been asleep for the last two days."

The icy road. The telephone pole. The throbbing in her head. Evelyn tried to sit up but fell right back onto the pillow.

"Just relax, now. I'm going to call the doctor and he'll be right in to see you."

As she listened to the squeaky sound of the rubber-soled shoes leaving the room, Evelyn remembered.

Clara.

CHAPTER 117

The carpeting was being steam-cleaned and the walls repainted in her office. It would be a few days yet before she would be able to settle back in there.

"Can I camp out with you again today?" Annabelle asked her friend as they left the conference room.

"*Mi casa es su casa,* honey." Constance smiled. "I won't be taking too much of a risk though, will I, hanging out with you?" she joked. "I guess nothing is going to happen to us right inside the Broadcast Center."

"Edgar Rivers probably thought the same thing," Annabelle answered.

Though it was still a bit early on the West Coast, Annabelle wanted to call Jerome's brother, offer her condolences, and see if there was anything she could do to help.

"I hope I didn't wake you," she apologized as Peter Henning answered the phone.

"No, not at all. I woke up early. I just can't sleep."

"That's understandable, Peter. I just wanted to tell you myself that I am so sorry about Jerome."

"I know you are, Annabelle. Thank you. I guess you know Jerome was crazy about you."

"I cared for him too, Peter. We're going to miss him, aren't we?"

She could hear the sound of an exhale as a cigarette was lit three thousand miles away.

"Yeah, we're going to miss him. And I hate it that Jerome and I hadn't seen as much of each other as we should have over these last years. I'm realizing there was a lot going on in Jerome's life that I knew nothing about."

"Anything I might be able to fill you in on?" Annabelle offered.

"Well, the police let me into the house to pick up some of Jerome's papers. I found a contract in one of his folders. It seems he had been writing a book."

"Yes, I knew Jerome had written something, but I didn't know he had a publishing contract for it already." Annabelle was momentarily disappointed that her friend hadn't confided in her.

"No, this isn't a contract with a publishing house," said Peter. "This is a contract with Linus Nazareth for ghostwriting a book for him. It's a confidentiality agreement."

After printing out her notes on Jerome's manuscript, Annabelle read them over.

She might as well start at the top and get the worst over with. She was on a fishing expedition. She didn't know exactly what she would find, or even what she was looking for. She only hoped she'd know when she heard it.

Linus was on the telephone when she arrived at his office. He looked up with annoyance as Annabelle planted herself at his door. She waited while he finished his conversation, determined not to let courtesy get in the way of what she had to do. Not apologizing for breathing down his neck, she walked into the office and sat down.

"Let me put my cards on the table, Linus," she began. "I know that Jerome was the ghostwriter of your book."

Smooth. He was very smooth. If the executive producer was upset by her announcement, he didn't show it.

"So what?" Linus leaned back in his chair. "That's no crime. But if someone had signed a legal contract not to reveal that he had been a ghostwriter for someone else's book, and had been paid accordingly for his work, the crime would be in that person making the revelation."

"How convenient if the ghostwriter dies, taking the secret with him," Annabelle blurted.

The executive producer's smug smile spoke volumes. "Look, Annabelle, I had nothing to do with Jerome's death or your problems."

"Or Edgar Rivers's murder?" Annabelle dared him, knowing she might have gone too far.

"Or Edgar Rivers's murder," he confirmed. "But I can't say it hasn't occurred to me that things are simpler for me with Jerome gone."

Disgusted, Annabelle rose to leave the office. Reaching the door, she turned.

"Well I know he wrote it, Linus. And if something were to happen to me, I have left word with someone else that Jerome wrote your book," she lied.

After Annabelle stalked away, Linus closed the door. He walked over to his bookcase and took the football helmet off the shelf, slipping it onto his head.

His secretary sat outside the office, listening to the rhythmic knocking as Linus banged his head against the office wall.

CHAPTER 118

Agents Lyons and McGillicuddy sat at the rear of the room, there to watch the results of their investigative handiwork. Up front, Dr. John Lee sat beside his attorney as Christopher Neuman pleaded his client's case before the federal magistrate.

"Dr. Lee is a respected doctor, journalist, and concerned citizen whose only aim was to inform the American public of the dangers of anthrax and the availability of that deadly substance. He should be released immediately, on his own recognizance."

The assistant U.S. attorney was having none of it. He stood to rebut. "On the contrary, Your Honor. There is probable cause to bring serious charges here. Dr. Lee unlawfully obtained a weapon of mass destruction, and the government will prove that the anthrax stolen by Dr. Lee was the same anthrax that infected Mr. Jerome Henning, killing him. We have a good-faith basis to believe that Dr. Lee is a killer. He is a danger to the public at large, and any potential witnesses in this case could also be in danger. The risk of flight is great."

In the current climate, the magistrate wasn't inclined to take any chances.

"Hold him," she ordered, "pending a detention hearing on Friday. A decision on bail will be made then."

Lee hung his head in despair and considered how his plans for glory had gone so terribly awry. He shouldn't be on his way to a six-by-ten cell with a bunk bed in a federal jail next to the Brooklyn Bridge in lower Manhattan. It was all a mistake. He hadn't meant for anyone to get hurt.

"Don't worry, John," his attorney tried to reassure him. "They have to prove that you intended to do something—that you intended to harm Jerome Henning." The lawyer patted Lee's arm. "Your intent was to educate the public, John, not to use anthrax as a weapon. The government is going to have a damn difficult case to make. Unless they can prove that you *intended* to do harm to Jerome Henning, you'll never face criminal conviction."

CHAPTER

119

Lauren and Gavin were out on shoots and Wayne was nowhere to be found, but Russ Parrish was in his office, watching a movie on his monitor. Meryl Streep performed her magic on the screen.

"Russ, can I talk to you for a minute?"

"I figured you would make your way in here sooner or later. Come on in, Annabelle." Russ clicked off the monitor. "Actually, I'm starving. Want to get some lunch? We can talk in the cafeteria. I have something I want to ask you about and something I want to confide in you as well."

Russ and Annabelle sat in a booth at Station Break, their bowls of lentil soup untouched on the table.

"I read over your shoulder yesterday . . . the stuff about me growing up poor and growing to love the good life, acquiring a cocaine addiction along the way," Russ said.

Annabelle answered with silence.

"Why were you writing that, Annabelle?"

She mentally debated if she should tell Russ about Jerome's manuscript. At this point, it made no sense to hold back the information, especially since she had already turned over her notes to the FBI. Jerome was dead and there was no secret to keep now.

"I was re-creating what I could remember of a manuscript that Jerome had been working on about behind-the-scenes kind of stuff at *KTA*," she explained.

Russ laughed with cynicism. "I gather it wasn't a valentine to our happy little broadcast."

"No. It wasn't."

"Did Jerome have a publisher for this manuscript?" he asked.

"No, not yet."

"Well, I guess I can be grateful for that," Russ said softly. "You know, Annabelle, I realize it sounds like I'm making excuses for myself, but it was Jerome who introduced me to cocaine."

"I'm sure he didn't stick it up your nose, Russ."

"True, but he was very generous with the stuff until I was nice and hooked. Then, when he got off it, he didn't want to have anything to do with me. He dropped me like a hot potato."

"That makes sense. Why would Jerome keep hanging out with an addict when he was trying to kick his own addiction?" Annabelle had no inclination to show Russ any sympathy.

"Maybe you're right, but I'll tell you one thing. If the tiny part I read about me is indicative of the type of hatchet job he was doing on other people in his book, there are lots of us who should be glad that Jerome Henning is dead—and worried that you could pick up his torch. You better be very careful, Annabelle."

CHAPTER

120

FROM: YELENA GREGORY

TO: ALL PERSONNEL

THERE WILL BE A FUNERAL SERVICE FOR EDGAR RIVERS THIS EVENING AT 7:00 P.M. AT THE CALVARY BAPTIST CHURCH IN THE BRONX. A VAN WILL BE LEAVING THE BROADCAST CENTER AT 6:00 P.M. TO TRANSPORT ANY EMPLOYEES WHO WISH TO ATTEND.

CHAPTER

121

"The chairman of Wellstone was taken off in handcuffs this morning. . . ."

Gavin's heart beat faster as he sat in the back of the crew car, listening to the report on the radio.

". . . faces possible imprisonment and multimillion-dollar fines for unloading Wellstone stock at a giant profit while having insider knowledge of confidential company developments."

As the radio report ended, the KEY sedan parked in an NYPD space near the entrance to the Columbia University Business School. Gavin walked ahead, while B.J. unloaded the camera gear.

He was killing two birds with one stone. Getting an interview for tomorrow morning's Wellstone scandal piece with one of the lawyers who worked on the congressional briefing books for the Securities and Exchange Commission investigations and, at the same time, ascertaining his own legal situation. He'd made a hefty profit on his Wellstone stock, but he had planned to sell it anyway, even before he'd gotten the early news. He could prove that if he had to.

The law professor and Gavin waited as B.J. unwound wires and set up lights. In the guise of small talk, Gavin took the opportunity to get in his burning question before the interviewee was miked.

"Go over it with me, will you, Roger?" Gavin asked. "Are there any exceptions to the insider trading rules? Could someone who had important nonpublic information ever sell his stock, take his profit, and still be within the limits of the law?"

The professor frowned. "It's a tricky question, and the courts have disagreed. But the rules permit someone to trade when it's clear that the information was not a factor in the decision to trade. For example, if the person had instructed his broker in advance to sell when the stock hit a certain price."

Gavin registered a mental *yes*!

He would be okay on this one.

CHAPTER

122

After lunch, the bulletin came from the Associated Press.

"Another anthrax death confirmed in New Jersey," Dominick O'Donnell shouted to the newsroom.

All hands clicked on their computers to bring up the story on their screens.

AN AUTOPSY PERFORMED ON A WOMAN NAMED CLARA ROMANSKI DETECTED THE PRESENCE OF *B. ANTHRACIS.* ROMANSKI WAS FOUND DEAD IN HER APARTMENT LAST WEEKEND. A FRIEND TOLD POLICE THAT ROMANSKI HAD BEEN A HOUSEKEEPER FOR 36-YEAR-OLD JEROME HENNING, A KEY NEWS PRODUCER WHO DIED ON SUNDAY, ANOTHER VICTIM OF ANTHRAX POISONING.

"Holy crap," Linus whistled.

"God help her," whispered Beth.

CHAPTER 123

Collateral damage. That's what Clara Romanski's death was: collateral damage. Like the civilians who were mistakenly killed in military battles or the pedestrians wounded in gang-war street fights. In conflicts, the innocent often got hurt. It was unfortunate, but it went with defending the territory.

Edgar Rivers was collateral damage too.

Not two, but three deaths now.

Soon to be four.

CHAPTER

124

Lauren had just returned from her shoot when Linus snagged her in the newsroom.

"This is a great opportunity for you, Lauren," he insisted. "We'll reschedule the consumer story you were slated to do tomorrow and run it later in the week. Go out to New Jersey and bring me back something we can promo as 'Terror in Maplewood.'"

Lauren needed no convincing. If she was ever to get Constance's job, she needed more hard news pieces under her belt.

"Who's my producer?"

"Annabelle Murphy."

As B.J. drove the car through the Lincoln Tunnel, Annabelle and Lauren discussed strategy. Lauren decided it was in her best interest to let Annabelle take the lead.

"Let's go into town and interview people on the street to get their reactions to what's happening in their usually peaceful suburb," Annabelle suggested, remembering the picturesque village that she had visited with Jerome. "B.J. can get some beauty shots of the Maplewood downtown area and the upscale homes."

Lauren nodded. "'Residents have chosen to live in this tree-lined community of snug homes and good schools thinking they were making a safe life for themselves and their children' type of thing?"

"Exactly," said Annabelle with gratitude that they were on the same page. Lauren may not have been at the top of Annabelle's favorite people list, but Annabelle was relieved that the reporter was smart enough to pick up immediately on the vision of what they were going for in the piece. Maybe Lauren wasn't the lightweight Jerome portrayed her as.

As Annabelle observed Lauren tapping her foot against the car floor mat, she realized Lauren might be nervous. This assignment was outside her usual reporting area.

Annabelle knew she had to focus on the piece and make sure they got the makings of a first-rate news story for tomorrow's show. This wasn't the time to pump Lauren for information or create an adversarial relationship. They had to work together this afternoon.

After the baby woke from his nap, the au pair changed his diaper and dressed him in his red snowsuit.

"Come here, Sandy. Come on, girl," she called in her thick accent. The long-haired golden retriever loped forward and waited patiently as the leash was clipped to her collar.

Once the baby was loaded into the stroller, the three headed down the hill for their afternoon walk to town. The walk broke up the long day, stuck in the house with a four-month-old for ten hours at a clip while the baby's parents were off at their offices. All these days were long, spent in an unfamiliar country with little companionship beside the television set. Soap operas and Oprah Winfrey. It wasn't what the au pair had envisioned when she signed on. She had thought living in America for a year would be much more thrilling than it had been so far. The most excitement had been when the police had come this past weekend to the house across the street where the man who died of anthrax had lived. And that was an excitement the au pair could do without.

Since the police had been there, she had watched the anthrax stories on the news that explained how the first apparent symptoms appeared days after exposure, and she had been wondering if she should tell the police what she had seen. But the police in her own country scared her and, it followed, the American police were scary as well.

The au pair didn't want any trouble.

It wasn't hard to find people who wanted to talk. Annabelle stood on the sidewalk in front of the Maple Leaf Diner and approached customers as they entered and exited.

"Hi, I'm Annabelle Murphy with KEY News. We're doing a story on the latest anthrax casualty. Would you be willing to answer a few questions for us?"

When the affirmative responses came, Lauren stepped in with her microphone and asked the questions while B.J. trained his camera on the faces.

"Of course, it scares me," answered a young mother as she straddled her toddler on her hip. "We moved out here last year from Manhattan to get away from terrorism. Now I'm worried that nowhere is safe. There's really nowhere to run."

Annabelle jotted down the words in her reporter's notebook, sure they'd want to use that sound bite in their piece.

The au pair stood on the corner and watched as the American news crew interviewed people in front of the diner. She didn't recognize any of them from television, but it was exciting nonetheless. At least she would have something to write home about tonight.

As she rolled the stroller back and forth in place, she wished that she could go forward and be interviewed and then see herself on television later. But she didn't know if that would be a good idea. Not only was she self-conscious about her heavy Irish accent but what would she really have to say that anyone would be interested in?

The baby began to fuss. As she searched for the pacifier in the stroller pocket, the idea occurred to her. Maybe there was a way to feel part of the excitement.

Within half an hour, Annabelle knew they had plenty of sound bites to choose from. She glanced at her watch. The sky was beginning to darken. They still had to get the B-roll of the town and swing by Essex Hills Hospital to get an exterior shot of the building. If they were to make it back to the Broadcast Center and get the script written in time for her to catch that van to Edgar's funeral, they had to get moving.

"I think we have enough here, don't you, Lauren?"

"Yes, we have some really good stuff." The reporter nodded. "But what about my stand-up?"

Not only knowing that the piece needed to illustrate

reporter involvement but positive that Lauren would want her "face time," Annabelle had anticipated the question.

"I was thinking that it would be good to shoot it in front of the train station up the block," she suggested. "You could say something about the New York City commuters who leave their families each day in the supposed safety of the suburbs only to find that they're as vulnerable here as anywhere else."

"Exactly what I was thinking," Lauren agreed.

It wasn't worth packing up the gear and driving the short distance to the train station. They could walk it. As they crossed the street, a young woman pushing a baby stroller approached.

"Excuse me."

Lauren glanced at the young woman but kept on walking. B.J. rolled his eyes at Lauren's single-mindedness and shrugged.

"It's all right. Go ahead, Beej. I'll be right behind you." Annabelle stopped and turned her attention to the wide-eyed female.

"Yes?"

"You're doing a story on anthrax, right?"

"Yes."

"I have something you might want to know."

Annabelle doubted it, but she waited.

"I work for a family who lives across the street from the

man who died from the anthrax. The Friday night before the man got sick, I saw something when I was walking the dog." The young woman glanced down at the golden retriever.

Annabelle's interest was piqued now. "What was it? What did you see?"

"I was walking Sandy, and I passed someone on the street near the man's house."

"A man or a woman?"

"It was dark and I really couldn't tell. Whoever it was had on pants and a heavy overcoat with the collar turned up. But when Sandy was done, I walked back up the hill, and I could see the person put something into the mailbox of the man who got anthrax."

"Did you tell the police this?"

The au pair shook her head. "At first, I didn't think anything of it. But then, when I saw on the news that the man across the street must have been exposed to the anthrax days before he got sick, I was afraid to tell the police."

Annabelle flipped to a clean page in her notebook.

"What is your name?" she asked.

The au pair looked nervous. "I don't want any trouble."

"The police should know about this," Annabelle urged.

Again, the girl shook her head.

"All right, but let me give you my card. If you think of anything else, will you please call me?" Annabelle scribbled her cell phone number on the back.

The young woman looked at the white card with the official KEY News logo.

"There was one other thing," she offered, feeling that she could trust this Annabelle Murphy, who wasn't making her feel trapped, this lady who was making her feel important and interesting.

"The person had on a baseball cap. I recognized the circles on it. It was from the Olympics."

CHAPTER 125

"Would you feel comfortable knowing that every e-mail you've ever written could wind up on the front page of *The New York Times?*" Yelena barked as she paced angrily across the office carpet. "That's what you should keep in the back of your mind, Gavin, when you put things in writing and send them over the Internet."

"*The New York Times* isn't monitoring my e-mails, Yelena." Gavin tried to remain calm as he sat in the hot seat.

"No, but KEY News has that right. It's printed in black and white in the policy on company computer use. How stupid could you be, Gavin, writing those interns like that?"

"I haven't done anything wrong, haven't written anything objectionable," he defended himself.

"You're right on the cusp, Gavin. I'm warning you. Lay off the interns. The last thing we need around here right now is a sexual harassment suit."

CHAPTER 126

Maybe that baby-sitter didn't want to come forward herself, but as long as Annabelle didn't reveal anything that could be used to trace the au pair's identity, there was nothing stopping Annabelle from telling Joe Connelly about the sighting of a person wearing an Olympics cap putting something in Jerome Henning's mailbox on the Friday night before he fell sick. Joe could let the police know. Annabelle didn't want to call them if she could help it.

As Lauren worked on her script, Annabelle walked down to Security, but Connelly was not in his office. She left him a note, saying that she needed to speak with him, and then went right back upstairs. The van was leaving in forty-five minutes, and she wanted to be on it.

If Lauren would just finish that script, Annabelle could polish it a bit, send it off for approval, and have Lauren record her track. Annabelle would leave all the videotapes with an editor to assemble tonight and come in extra early in the morning to look the package over.

She was running too fast, trying to do too much, and she knew it. That's when your family life suffered because your husband and children were neglected. That's when your professional life became unhinged. That's when you made mistakes.

Annabelle took the elevator to go back upstairs. One floor up, the car stopped and Gavin Winston got on beside her.

"Watch out, Annabelle. Big Brother's watching," the gray-haired correspondent grumbled. "Yelena is scouring our e-mails."

"No way," Annabelle gasped, unbelieving. The invasion of privacy was too disgusting to digest. "What are you talking about, Gavin?"

"I don't want to get into the specifics," he said shortly, "but be forewarned. Your e-mails aren't private."

If Gavin was right, KEY News wasn't the place she hoped it was. As she got off the elevator, Annabelle tried to remember if she had sent any e-mails that she wouldn't want others to read. She must have.

CHAPTER 127

As she scanned the inside of the blue van, Annabelle was disappointed but not surprised. While most of the seats were occupied, the riders were almost all people she recognized as cafeteria or maintenance workers. The only other news staffers who were bothering to attend Edgar's service were Constance and Yelena. The three of them sat together in seats at the front.

The van turned from Fifty-seventh Street onto the ramp for the West Side Highway and inched along in the rush-hour traffic going north toward the George Washington Bridge. While their destination was only ten miles away, as the crow flies, they'd need most of the allotted hour for travel time.

The conversation turned to the latest anthrax developments. Annabelle recounted her visit to Maplewood and confided the information she had gotten from the baby-sitter.

"Well, that's something that really might help the police," Yelena said, her eyebrow arching.

Annabelle nodded. "I went down to tell Joe Connelly, but I missed him. Don't worry, though. I'll make sure I get the information to him."

The velvet-padded pews of Calvary Baptist Church were packed for Edgar Rivers's Going Home Celebration, a testimony to the life and faith of a hardworking, hard-praying man.

Women dressed in white uniforms and caps, looking more like nurses than ushers, stood at the back of the church and escorted mourners up the right aisle to view the open casket, which was positioned directly below the pulpit. Annabelle said a silent prayer as she gazed down at Edgar, his face serene now, his still hands folded across his chest. As she turned and walked past the front pew, Annabelle recognized the woman and the two little boys who had come to visit Edgar in the cafeteria the morning that turned out to be the last day of Edgar Rivers's life. Was that only Friday? It seemed like such a long time ago. The woman looked up and smiled with sadness as her red-rimmed eyes met Annabelle's.

"Please be seated. The service is about to begin," whispered one of the ushers. Annabelle, Constance, and Yelena were directed down the left aisle to a half-full pew near the back of the church. As she took her seat, Annabelle heard a disturbing cranking sound; the pillow that propped up Edgar's head was being lowered and the coffin being closed.

The organist began to play. Annabelle counted the twenty-six choir members, dressed in blue-and-white robes, who stood in three tiers at the right front of the church, their beautiful voices raised in song. Readings from scripture were interspersed with spirited choral salutes. The black-robed minister mounted the pulpit, high above the congregation at the center of attention.

"Edgar Rivers was a good man, a kind man, a giving man, devoted to his sister, Ruby, and her boys, Freddie and Willie. Let me hear an Amen," the preacher encouraged.

"Amen," came the shouts from the pews.

"Brother Edgar was a hardworking man, a churchgoing man, a God-loving man."

"That's right," one of the choristers agreed. "Alleluia."

Perspiring in November, the minister wiped his brow with a black terry washcloth as he poured his heart and soul into the sermon. The eulogy continued in a rising synergy, the minister and the congregation each energized by the other.

As the service concluded, Annabelle listened to the soloist who stepped forward to sing the verse of a song she'd never heard before. The chorus and the congregation, their bodies swaying left and right, and hands clapping to the beat, answered with the uplifting, promising response of *"He's an On Time God."*

Annabelle couldn't help but wonder where God had been when Edgar met his end. He must have been running behind schedule. Come to think of it, where had God been lately? Jerome's death, anthrax, September 11, Mike's depression. Annabelle wanted to believe that God would be there "right on time," but that was a tough sell right now.

Edgar's sister and her sons were standing in the church vestibule, greeting people and accepting condolences. Annabelle introduced herself.

"Yes, I remember you. You're the nice lady from the cafeteria. Edgar told me that morning that you were one of the few people who gave him the time of day."

Feeling embarrassed and wanting to put a better face on her colleagues, Annabelle hastily continued with introductions. "This is Constance Young," she said, as Ruby extended her hand to the *KTA* host.

"Oh yes. I recognize you."

"I'm sorry for your loss," Constance answered. "We'll miss Edgar. He was a very nice person to have around every day."

Ruby's dark eyes glistened. "Don't I know that. I don't know what my boys and I are going to do without him."

There was an uneasy pause.

Annabelle stepped in to fill the gap. "And this is Yelena Gregory, the president of KEY News. She had a van chartered to bring the people up here from the Broadcast Center today."

"Thank you for coming. That was very nice of you," Ruby responded, turning to Yelena. "With all those budget cuts Edgar was always talking about, it was very nice of you to do that. And thank you for sending the flowers."

"It was the least we could do," said Yelena.

As the KEY newswomen began to move away, Ruby turned to Annabelle. "Will you be able to come to the graveside service tomorrow morning?" she asked.

Annabelle hadn't been planning on it. "At what time?" she asked politely.

"Nine o'clock, right here in the cemetery behind the church."

"I'm so sorry, but I don't think so. I have to be at work then. I hope you understand. It's hard to get away in the mornings."

"Sure, I understand," said Ruby, looking disappointed. "It's hard to get away."

CHAPTER

128

By the time the van had dropped everyone back at the Broadcast Center and Annabelle splurged on a cab to take her down to the Village, stopping to get the pumpkin pie the twins needed for the class Thanksgiving party, it was after nine o'clock. When she walked in the front door, the apartment was quiet. The kids were already in bed, and Mike was sleeping on the couch in the living room.

Annabelle hung her beaver jacket on the back of the kitchen chair, kicked off her shoes, and opened the refrigerator. The sparsely occupied shelves were a reminder that she had to get to the market tomorrow and do some real shopping. The day before Thanksgiving would be a zoo at the grocery store.

Deciding to scramble some eggs, she pulled the frying pan from the drawer. The clatter of pans woke Mike, who walked into the kitchen.

"I'm sorry, honey," she apologized. "I didn't mean to wake you."

"How was the funeral?"

Annabelle whisked the eggs in a mixing bowl. "Actually, very nice as those things go. It had lots of spirit to it." She poured the yellow mixture into the pan. "How was your day?"

"Okay, but I'm beat for some reason. I couldn't even muster the energy to give the kids a bath tonight."

Annabelle looked at her husband with concern.

"You should take it easy, Mike. You don't want to overdo it." She kissed him on the cheek. "And don't worry about the baths. The kids can live for one night without them."

"I'll be right behind you, sweetheart," said Annabelle as she set the frying pan in the sink to soak. "I'm just going to wipe up around here and then I'm turning in early too."

She watched as Mike walked to the bedroom, hoping he wasn't slipping backwards again. With all that had been happening at work, maybe she had been putting too much pressure on him, thrusting the child care on him too quickly. Tomorrow would be better, she resolved. She would come right home after work and a quick-as-possible trip to the supermarket.

The kitchen straightened, Annabelle switched off the overhead fixture and headed toward the twins' room. As she stood in the doorway, the light from the hallway cast a soft glow on their peaceful faces. For the umpteenth time, her heart filled with the love and wonder of having them and ached at the fact that she hadn't even spoken to her children today. They'd been asleep when she left in the morning, and they were asleep now.

She tiptoed inside and kissed Tara on the forehead, tucking the covers around her little body. Thomas was sucking his thumb again, Annabelle observed with resignation, as she gently pulled his soft hand away from his mouth.

Annabelle didn't see the other hand, warm beneath the covers, or the small black lesion that grew on the tip of one of Thomas's fingers.

CHAPTER 129

He liked working the night shift, and he liked having his master key. He could snoop around to his heart's content. Sometimes there were prizes ripe for the picking. He rationalized that the office supplies he filched supplemented the measly salary he was earning for the unpleasant job of cleaning up after other people's messes. At least KEY was paying for the notebooks and pens and folders that his kids used at school.

He pushed his garbage container down the long ramp, stopping at a closet he hadn't tried before. He unlocked the heavy door and felt for the light switch.

"Hey, look at all this old Olympic stuff."

The custodian dug through the pile of baseball caps and T-shirts in the cartons strewn around the floor. A rack held ski parkas emblazoned with the snow flower emblem of the 1998 Olympics held in Nagano, Japan. He searched until he found one marked XXL and folded it up. That would fit him just fine. Maybe he should pick one up for his brother too.

As he pushed back the jackets, the gleam of reflected glass caught his eye.

What were test tubes doing in here?

"High winds and driving rains will be reaching our area in a few hours."

The weather segment on the local eleven o'clock news was wrapping up when Joe Connelly's home phone rang.

One of the cleaning crew had opened a little-used supply closet in the basement of the Broadcast Center and found a box of protective gloves and a junior chemistry set.

"Keep the door shut and don't let anyone near that closet," Joe ordered. "I'm coming in. And don't let that custodian go home."

Perspiration glistened on the janitor's brow.

"I thought I should let Security know, Mr. Connelly. With all the anthrax stuff that has been happening around here and all."

"You did the right thing, Mickey. But if you took anything from that closet, I suggest you hand it over," Joe said knowingly. "No questions asked. You wouldn't want to risk anything happening to you, would you?"

Joe called his connection at the local police precinct. It would be important to maintain the chain of evidence.

"The chemistry set and protective gloves are evidence, to my mind, that whoever killed Jerome Henning may have been cooking things up in that closet. I have a wireless camera we can install here and see what we catch."

Joe was going to keep KEY out of it this time. They didn't

need any more panic at the Broadcast Center. He could take care of the problem on his own.

You couldn't trust people to keep their mouths shut.

Surveillance cameras came in all shapes and sizes. They could be hidden almost anywhere, in pencil sharpeners or smoke detectors or sprinkler heads. Joe selected a miniature camera and personally escorted the technician down to the basement to set it up.

"What kind of field of view do you want?" the tech asked. "Wide-angle to pick up as much as you can, or narrow to pick up the details?"

Joe thought a minute before responding.

"Go with the narrow, Milt," he decided. "We want to see the face of whoever comes to this closet."

WEDNESDAY

NOVEMBER 26

CHAPTER

130

Annabelle awoke to the sound of wind and rain rattling against the window glass. She reached over to switch off the alarm, hoping to spare Mike another early wake-up. Managing to pick out her clothes in the dark, she crept from the bedroom as her husband slept.

The hot shower felt good until the water hit the cut on her knee. She gingerly held the washcloth in her damaged hands, instant reminders of the bus accident. She turned off the showerhead and toweled off carefully, dressing quickly in the unlit living room.

As she waited for water to boil for the container of tea she would take with her on the cab ride, Annabelle looked out the window to Perry Street. In the light of the streetlamps, she could see blustering rain pounding on the pavement below. Garbage cans were tipped over, spilling their contents onto the slick sidewalk. There were no birds sitting on the fire escapes this morning.

The nor'easter was really blowing in. It had been a good call to do the broadcast in the studio today.

CHAPTER

131

It had to be done early, before the building filled with people for the day shift, while there was still a chance to go and clean out the storage closet undetected. The *KTA* staffers were straggling in already. There was no time to waste.

The chemistry set and the gloves could prove to be links to Jerome Henning's and Clara Romanski's deaths. If someone discovered them hidden at the back of the closet, the police would soon be alerted. Law enforcement, with all its sophisticated testing abilities, would surely pick up something. Traces of anthrax, a strand of hair, a fingerprint left behind.

There was no one in the hallway that led to the basement ramp.

CHAPTER

132

After grabbing a few hours' sleep in the dressing room, Joe arose, freshened up, and headed downstairs to the security office. As he checked the monitor for the camera trained on the basement storage closet, he felt the anger rise within him.

Damn it. The camera wasn't working.

"Didn't anyone notice this?" he growled. The tired overnight guards looked at the screen, their expressions as blank as the monitor.

Joe grabbed the telephone to call the technician.

"I'll meet you down there myself," he declared. "Pronto."

CHAPTER

133

Someone had been in here since the last time. The coats were pushed back on the rack, the cartons on the floor rearranged. But the chemistry set still sat on the abandoned typewriter table, the box of nitrile gloves beside it.

The evidence was dropped into a thick plastic bag as noises were heard coming from the other side of the door.

The aluminum ladder scraped against the concrete floor as the technician positioned it under the ceiling fire sprinkler opposite the storage closet.

"We better get it right this time, Milt," the security chief ordered. "I don't want to miss anything."

"I don't know what happened, Joe," apologized the technician as he climbed the ladder. "This is a wireless camera, though, and you know the problems we have with these things."

Joe craned his neck to watch the tinkering. "Well, I hope we won't have to depend on it for too long but, in the meantime, make sure the damn thing works."

An ear was pressed against the closet door, listening to the conversation out in the hall.

Be quiet. Be very quiet. Just wait and listen. Don't panic.

After a few minutes, something scraped against the floor again.

"That should do it, Joe," said one of the voices.

"Thanks, Milt" was the response. "Now let's see what we catch."

The sound of the footsteps grew fainter until there was silence.

If a camera was pointed at the door, it would give it all away. If escape was possible, it had to be done quickly and anonymously.

Grabbing the plastic bag and a large ski parka from the rack, the killer slipped on the jacket and pulled up the hood, holding the edges close to cover the face.

"Look at that, will ya?" cried the guard as he watched the monitor in the security command post.

He jumped from his chair and ran to the door, bumping into the returning Joe Connelly. "What's going on?" the security chief asked.

"Somebody just came out of that closet, Joe."

"All right. That's good. We have it on tape."

"No. We won't be able to tell who it is. The face was covered."

When the men ran together to the basement, they found a discarded Olympics ski jacket at the bottom of the ramp.

CHAPTER 134

The editor had done an excellent job with the "Terror in Maplewood" piece. Annabelle screened the video package and grudgingly admitted to herself that Lauren looked and sounded great in her on-camera bridge. The woman had a certain quality that left Annabelle with little doubt Lauren could go far in broadcast journalism.

As Annabelle slid the tape from the video deck, she hoped that Linus wasn't in yet and that Dominick would be the one to give final approval on the piece. That way she would be sure to get an honest opinion of the work. Linus's view was biased when it came to Lauren.

Whoever it came from, once Annabelle got the piece approval, the next thing on her agenda was to find Joe Connelly and tell him what the au pair had told her about the baseball cap-wearing mail deliverer.

CHAPTER 135

He'd be damned if the suspect would get out of the Broadcast Center.

"We're locking this place down," Joe announced. "Alert all the exits. No one is to enter or leave the building."

As the word went out to the security guards, Joe strode

up to the main lobby, where the public address system was located. He composed his statement in his mind, knowing that the words he chose would be important. He didn't want to cause mass panic.

"We have an emergency in the building that is requiring us not to let anyone enter or leave at this time. Please be assured that you are in no danger. Stand by your computers for further information."

He hung up the mouthpiece and immediately picked up the telephone at the main desk. Joe knew the NYPD number by heart. After he informed his contact of what had happened, he made his suggestion.

"I think you guys should bring in a K-9 team."

The president of KEY News was tapping against the lobby's plate-glass window.

"It's all right, Roberto. Let her in," Joe said to the guard.

"What's going on here?" Yelena demanded as she shook out her umbrella.

"There's a good chance that our anthrax buddy is right here in the building." The security chief told her about the camera installed overnight on the suspicious closet and the discarded ski-parka disguise.

"Finding someone with that little to go on in this huge

building could be like finding a needle in a haystack," Yelena observed.

When informed of the police dog team that was on its way, she nodded. "All right, but keep that animal away from me. I can't stand dogs."

CHAPTER 136

"That's a helluva thing to tell us two minutes before we air," griped Linus as he walked into the control room. "What the hell is going on around here?"

As Constance and Harry appeared on the television screen, welcoming the audience to *KEY to America,* Linus picked up the phone and called Yelena. Her explanation was fine, as far as it went. He needed to assign a producer to keep on top of this story as the broadcast aired. If an arrest was made, Linus wanted to beat the competition in reporting it.

"Who's available, Dominick?" he asked the senior producer sitting next to him at the console.

"Annabelle Murphy is free. Her piece is all done."

CHAPTER 137

Annabelle took the call informing her of her new assignment. Her first step should be to talk to Joe Connelly.

"Annabelle, line three," Wayne called across the newsroom.

She snatched up the receiver. "Annabelle Murphy."

"Annabelle, it's me."

"Oh, hi, Mike. What's up?"

He could tell by her clipped tone that she was under pressure there.

"I hate to bother you with this, honey. But Thomas has this weird scab on his hand."

"What does it look like?" she asked as the hairs on her arms raised.

"It's black, like coal."

Sweet Jesus. She couldn't get out of the building!

Annabelle ached to fly out the door and rush downtown. She wanted to meet them at the hospital emergency room, talk to the doctors, hold her son's hand. If something happened to Thomas, she would never, ever forgive herself. Tears welled in her eyes.

Yet she knew, instinctively, that she had to stay calm. Her panic wouldn't help her little boy. What would help was clear thinking. She tried to remember the research she'd done for the Lee piece. The coal-like scab signaled cutaneous anthrax, the less deadly form. *Please, dear God, please, the much more treatable form.*

If the treatment came in time.

CHAPTER 138

The moment the parents left the house to catch the train into the city, the baby-sitter switched on the television set. While the baby's bottle heated, she watched as the pretty blond lady introduced the story.

"There's been another anthrax death in a prosperous New Jersey suburb. While investigators have arrested former KEY Medical Correspondent John Lee in connection with anthrax allegedly obtained illegally, town residents are worried. *KEY to America* correspondent Lauren Adams has more about the terror in Maplewood."

The au pair stared as the video showed so many of the places she recognized from her walks around town with the baby. She listened to the people she had seen being interviewed in front of the diner. She wished that she could have been one of those people, who now had something to tell their friends. She envied them. They were famous now.

When the video story ended, too quickly as far as she was concerned, the *KTA* host and the reporter the au pair recognized from yesterday came back on camera in the studio, conversing about the anthrax cases and the fear that had begun to grip the town.

The young Irish woman went to her purse, taking the business card from her wallet. As she studied the white card, she thought perhaps she should call Annabelle Murphy and tell her the other thing she remembered. But as she went to the phone, the baby cried, diverting her attention back to the job for which she was so poorly paid.

CHAPTER

139

The yellow Labrador retriever, along with her handler and other police officers, was escorted down to the basement ramp. The silver ski jacket was held to the dog's nose.

"Every person's scent is as unique as a fingerprint. Health, ethnic origin, the type of food the person eats, and the soap and perfumes he wears all make up the individual's scent," explained the handler. "But this could be a tough one. From what you say, this jacket wasn't worn for very long. We should probably go into the closet too and let Duchess try to catch the scent in there as well."

"What about the possibility of anthrax exposure?" asked Joe.

"You stay back," instructed the handler. "We've all been vaccinated."

"Even the dog?"

He patted Duchess on her head. "Though we're concerned about the risk, we know that dogs are about five hundred to a thousand times less likely than humans to develop an anthrax infection."

CHAPTER

140

Annabelle checked to make sure that her cell phone was on. Mike would call her on it as soon as he had some news. There was absolutely nothing she could do to help Thomas right now. She had to keep busy, keep her mind off her little boy, or she would go insane.

If they found the murderer in the building, Annabelle wanted to be there for it. They'd have to pull her off the monster. Her fists clenched at the thought of the miserable wretch who had hurt her son.

Suddenly, she was glad to have this assignment.

"Mr. Connelly isn't in the office."

"This is Annabelle Murphy. It's urgent that I speak with him."

"We can beep him, but it might be a while before he gets back to you. He's with the police K-9 unit."

Annabelle hung up the phone. So they were using dogs to try to track the killer. Her professional mind automatically went into gear.

She had better get pictures of that.

"No, I don't know exactly where they are," admitted Annabelle. "We'll just have to scout around until we find them."

"All right," said the cameraman. "I'll meet you in the lobby in five minutes."

Annabelle grabbed her notebook and pen and was heading out of the newsroom when another call came in for her. It was Ruby, Edgar's sister.

"I just wanted to tell you that Edgar's graveside service has been postponed because of the bad weather out there, in case you might want to come."

Annabelle wanted to scream. Sad as it was, Edgar's burial was the last thing on her mind this morning. "Thank you for telling me, Ruby," she managed to answer. "When you know the rescheduled time, let me know. If I'm not here, just leave it on my voice mail, all right?"

She wanted to get off the phone, but Ruby had more to get off her chest.

"It was awfully nice of you all to come to the Going Home Celebration last night. I have to admit, I was kinda surprised that the big boss came and paid for that van. Edgar told me she was mighty cheap."

Where the heck was that coming from? "Oh, you mean cheap with the budget cuts?" Annabelle asked. "That's just Yelena's job. She has to enforce those things."

"That's what Edgar said too. But he couldn't believe it when he caught the big boss one day taking sugar from the cafeteria. Doing your job is one thing, being cheap is another."

CHAPTER 141

Russ felt his stomach growl. He still had more than half an hour before his segment was scheduled. Since leaving the building to go up to the corner deli was out, he could grab something cold off the guests' table in the greenroom or go downstairs to the cafeteria and get what he was really in the mood for, a bowl of hot, creamy oatmeal.

As he approached the entrance to Station Break, he saw the dog sniffing along the hallway floor.

"Wherever a person goes, whether he sits, stands, walks, runs, even swims, he sheds thousands of minute particles of skin," the handler explained for Joe's benefit as both kept their eyes on the retriever. "These rafts of skin contain the person's individual genetic scent composition. The more contamination that occurs in an area, though, the more difficult it is for the dog to work the available scent."

"So this guy walking toward us is going to foul things up, right?" Joe observed as Russ approached them.

"It ain't gonna help."

"Go back, sir. This is an investigation area," ordered the police officer, waving Russ away.

Russ was only too happy to comply. If that dog sniffed its way to his desk, he was going to be in big trouble. He had to get that powder out of his desk, out of the Broadcast Center.

CHAPTER 142

As she walked to the lobby to meet B.J., Annabelle recalled the twenty dollars she had lent Yelena the day the ATM was down. Twenty dollars perhaps simply forgotten with all that Yelena had on her mind. Annabelle had certainly forgotten about it herself until now. But Ruby's remark about Yelena's cheapness had made her remember.

How odd it was for someone, especially of Yelena's stature, to pilfer a cup of sugar. But further reflection about her boss and her motives was diverted as Annabelle spotted the cameraman waiting for her, ready to track down the K-9 team.

It didn't take long to find them.

The dog and its entourage were coming down the hallway toward the lobby.

B.J. switched his camera on and managed to get some video before the cops shooed him away.

"Joe, can I talk to you a minute?" Annabelle called to the security chief.

He shook his head. "Not now, Annabelle."

"It's important, Joe," she insisted.

"All right, but be quick about it," he said as he came toward her.

The retriever was leading the handler to the revolving door out to the street.

"Christ, if the suspect got outside, we're dead." The security chief groaned as he watched the dog circling in confusion.

"Joe, I just wanted to let you know about something I heard in Maplewood yesterday when we were out there for a shoot." Annabelle hurriedly recounted the story the au pair had told her.

"All right, I'll let the cops know," he responded as he turned his attention back to the dog.

"And, Joe," Annabelle said, as she took hold of his arm, "my son may have been exposed too." She gave him the details of what she knew so far about Thomas.

The security chief looked stricken.

"Can't you let me out of here, Joe?" she tried.

"I'm sorry, Annabelle. No exceptions."

Thinking her cooperation with him should at least earn some reciprocal information for her story, Annabelle continued, "All right, but I've got to do this story for the show, Joe. What can you tell me about what's happening here?"

"Sorry again, Annabelle. I would help you if I could, but there's nothing I can say right now."

CHAPTER

143

The second his movie segment interview with Harry finished at the end of the first hour of the broadcast, Russ clipped off his microphone and headed up to his office. He took the envelope from the bottom drawer of his desk and stuffed it in his raincoat pocket.

The main entrances might be blocked, but there were other ways out of the Broadcast Center.

If he escaped this time, Russ vowed he was going to clean up his act.

Gavin looked over the copy he was about to deliver on the Wellstone investigation. As he waited while the microphone was clipped to the lapel of his suit's soft jacket, he wondered how much longer he really wanted to continue in this business. Getting up most mornings at an ungodly hour, being under pressure to perform, enduring Linus's insults and tirades, and, now, the aspersions cast upon him by Yelena, assailing his character.

He didn't need this anymore. He had enough money, his retirement fund was fat. He could get a part-time teaching position at a university if he wanted to make sure that he would have breaks from Marguerite's harping. Yes, a college would be a good place to be. All those young, pretty coeds looking up to him.

He should get out while the going was still good.

CHAPTER 144

Annabelle's cell phone pulsed. With shaking hands, she flipped it open.

"Mike?" she answered anxiously.

"They aren't even waiting for the test results, Annabelle. They've already started Thomas on Cipro."

"What do the doctors say?"

"Eighty percent of cutaneous anthrax cases recover."

There was a long silence. Neither one of them would speak of the other 20 percent.

"Annabelle?"

"Yes, I'm here."

"Look, sweetheart, *all* that matters is Thomas getting well and you staying safe. Everything is going to be all right. I promise."

Annabelle hung on to the phone, fighting back tears and clinging to her husband's reassurance and strength. For the first time in these many months, she really started to sense that Mike was going to be okay.

CHAPTER 145

As Russ pushed through the heavy metal door, the red light flashed from the board in the security office.

"The alarm is blinking at the rear emergency exit on Fifty-sixth Street," the guard yelled at his colleague. "I'm running out there. You call Joe and let him know."

The guard pushed through the emergency door into the torrential rain. He looked from side to side and randomly decided to run toward Tenth Avenue. Squinting through the downpour, he searched fruitlessly.

It was too late.

"Damn it!" Joe hissed.

The dog was coming up empty, losing the track in the lobby, the rain washing away the possibility of following the scent outside and, now, someone had escaped through the back of building.

"Let's see if we can get prints off that emergency door," offered the cop.

CHAPTER 146

She tried to push thoughts of Thomas away and concentrate on the task at hand. If Joe, with his law enforcement background, wasn't going to share any information, perhaps Yelena, with her journalistic bent, would be more forthcoming. Yelena would understand that Annabelle needed to know the facts in order to report the story of what was happening in the Broadcast Center this morning.

Yelena saw her right away.

"They found some things in a storage closet downstairs that look suspicious. A chemistry set and a box of gloves," the president explained. "Joe had a camera trained on the closet. It caught someone running away. The dog is trying to pick up the scent from a jacket they found thrown aside near the closet. If you want," Yelena offered, "I'll take you down and show you the closet."

"Great, let me call my cameraman," said Annabelle.

Yelena glanced at the watch on her wrist. "I'm running behind and don't have the time to wait. Let me take you down there quickly and just show you where it is. You can call the cameraman from there and direct him down to meet you."

"Sounds like a plan, Yelena. Thank you for being so forthcoming," said Annabelle. "I really appreciate it."

"Just as long as I don't run into that police dog."

Annabelle looked at her quizzically.

"I'm allergic to dogs."

CHAPTER 147

As they reached the top of the basement ramp, Annabelle felt the vibration and pulled the cell phone from her pocket.

"Excuse me, Yelena, but I have to answer this. It might be my husband." She paused as she opened the phone. "Mike?"

"No. It's me, Colleen, the au pair from Maplewood. I talked to you yesterday?"

"Oh yes. I'm sorry, but I'm very busy right now. Can you give me your phone number and I'll call you back?" Annabelle felt for her pen.

The younger woman hesitated. "No, I don't think that

would be a good idea. But you told me to call if I remembered anything else."

"Okay, go ahead." Annabelle tried to be patient.

"It may be nothing, but I remembered that the person sneezed a few times after coming near the dog. Does that help?"

CHAPTER 148

Yelena waited as Annabelle took her phone call and considered the situation.

The bag with the chemistry set and gloves had gone the way of the knife that had killed Edgar Rivers, tossed deep into a garbage container several blocks away. The chances were next to nil that it would be found amid the tons of garbage discarded and hauled away in New York City each day. Both copies of Jerome's manuscript had been deposited in the apartment incinerator.

With no other evidence to speak of, this case could turn into a dead end for the police and FBI. Just as the post–September 11 anthrax cases had at the other networks.

All that remained was making sure Jerome Henning's vile portrayal of KEY News never saw the light of day, in any form. The manuscript was the reason this whole nightmare had been necessary.

Thank God she had been in the practice of monitoring e-mails or she might not have known about the manuscript until it was too late. Jerome would have published his book, and KEY News would have become a byword for scandal, a laughingstock.

That couldn't happen. She had worked too hard, had too much invested. Her legacy would not be destroyed. Yelena would do anything to protect her "baby." KEY News was all she had.

Annabelle presented the final worry. Though the FBI had Annabelle's notes on the manuscript, Yelena wasn't that concerned, especially since she wasn't listed in them and thus wasn't implicated as a suspect. Those agents weren't going to be writing any books. But Annabelle could get the bright idea to re-create Jerome's book herself. That was a chance that just couldn't be taken.

Annabelle had to be taken care of—before they reached the closet with its security camera. She could take Annabelle on with all the strength of a lioness protecting her cub. She didn't need a weapon other than her bare hands and the uncanny strength that came with desperation.

CHAPTER 149

Annabelle's mind fired rapidly as she made the terrifying connections.

Yelena was allergic to dogs. Yelena had taken sugar from the cafeteria, where poor Edgar might have seen her. Yelena was monitoring e-mails, and Jerome had e-mailed Annabelle many times about his manuscript.

Was Yelena the one who had killed Jerome and Edgar and that other poor woman in New Jersey? Was Yelena responsible for the fact that Annabelle's precious little boy was lying in a bed downtown at St. Vincent's with cutaneous anthrax?

Her fear turning into anger, Annabelle spun to face her enemy just as she felt Yelena's strong hands wrap around her neck.

CHAPTER 150

With only half an hour left in the show, Linus was pacing in the control room.

"Are we going to have something on the lockdown or not?" the executive producer demanded. "Why the hell hasn't Annabelle let us know where we stand?"

"I'll try to find her, Linus," offered Beth, picking up the phone.

CHAPTER 151

The cell phone flew through the air as she felt Yelena propel her against the industrial-size sink in the maintenance alcove at the top of the basement ramp. As Yelena's grasp tightened around her neck, Annabelle flailed, struggling amid the brooms and mops. Yelena outweighed her by a good forty pounds. Annabelle wasn't going to be able to beat her with the sheer force of her strength.

She had nothing to fight with except the pen she grasped in her fist. As she choked, Annabelle thought of Thomas and found the strength to jam the pen upward, hitting Yelena in the side of the neck.

In the studio, the restaurant chef was demonstrating how to carve a turkey for the viewers at home.

Harry popped a slice into his mouth. "It's delicious," he proclaimed, "but my knife never cuts so thin."

"God damn it," exclaimed Linus as he watched the monitor in the control room. "To hell with the turkey, I want the sniffing dog. Where the hell is Annabelle?"

As the pen hit her neck, Yelena's grip loosened and she fell backward. Annabelle pulled away, trying to scramble out of the alcove. When she reached the ramp, she looked out. The area was empty, but she called for help anyway.

"Nobody's going to hear you, Annabelle," Yelena hissed as she struggled to regain her footing and lunged forward.

"I don't know where she is, Beth," said B.J. into the phone. "The last I saw her was in the lobby about half an hour ago. But I have the video of the canine unit if you want it."

As she felt Yelena pulling her back into the alcove, Annabelle remembered the security camera. If she could just get the dozen yards or so to the closet, the security camera would see her. She could signal for help.

"You aren't going to get away with this," she whispered hoarsely, trying to distract Yelena.

"I think I will. They'll find you dead later, just like they did Edgar Rivers. And this sink here will work out just fine. I can wash the fingerprints from your neck after I kill you with my bare hands."

"Over an unpublished manuscript? What's the matter with you? It's just a job, Yelena."

"Wrong, Annabelle. It's my whole life."

Joe went back to his office, feeling defeated. He had missed his chance. The "hammer team" would be coming in a little while to check out the storage closet, but Joe was sure that the evidence was gone now.

With resignation, he ordered the exits reopened, sent out a companywide e-mail announcing that Broadcast Center employees could once again come and go as they pleased, and then sat, staring morosely at the monitor that displayed the closet door.

Thomas. Thomas. She had to get to Thomas. She had to get to her little boy.

"You twisted psychopath. My son is in the hospital because of you." Annabelle spat in her face. Yelena squeezed her eyes shut against the saliva, giving her just the moments she needed.

The mop was nearby. Annabelle managed to wrap her

hand around the handle and pull it toward her. Again, she thrust a projectile into Yelena and, this time, Annabelle was able to run.

Down the ramp, down to the closet, with Yelena following.

As the broadcast ended, Linus ordered with disgust, "When Annabelle does show up, send her in to see me. She better have a damn good explanation."

Annabelle heard the heavy footsteps pounding down the ramp behind her. In Yelena's blind rage she must have forgotten about the security camera, thought Annabelle as she ran toward the closet. Running for her life, for Mike, for the children.

Tara and Thomas, so young and innocent, so needing their mother. At the thought of Thomas and the anthrax that was infecting his small body, Annabelle felt her injured knee give way beneath her. She stumbled forward, crashing to the hard floor. Wincing, she tried to right herself again, as Yelena was given the precious moments needed to catch up.

Annabelle felt the crazed woman bearing down on her from behind, grabbing at her waist. As Yelena fought to pull her back, Annabelle scrambled on her stomach, using all her strength to inch forward.

Closer. A little closer to the closet.

Please, let me get there. Please, please, please, let someone be watching.

The camera's narrow view caught a limited picture, a raised fist, the back of a head. But it was enough to send Joe Connelly and his guards rushing downstairs.

EPILOGUE

Thanksgiving Day, November 27

"We're missing the parade, Mommy," whined the tiny figure in the hospital bed.

"No, we're not. We're watching it on TV."

"That's not the same," said Thomas, pouting.

"Next year, honey. Next year. I promise." Annabelle closed her eyes and kissed the child's forehead, thanking God that there would be a next year. The doctors were confident Thomas was going to make a full recovery.

"Look, Thomas, there's Clifford the Big Red Dog." Annabelle pointed to the television set mounted on the wall of the hospital room.

The child was diverted from his disappointment as he counted the giant balloons that floated down the parade route. Yesterday's storm had left a crystal clear morning sky in its wake, a perfect bright blue background for the vibrant balloons. Clowns ran in circles, stars waved from floats, cheerleaders cavorted, and marching bands played—it all seemed to Annabelle to be a celebration of the fact that her little boy was going to be all right.

The turtleneck she wore covered the bruises on her neck. Yelena was in police custody, and the incredulity that she had snapped so completely and inexorably was already giving way to intense speculation on who would succeed her as president of KEY News. Mental illness, a menopausal breakdown, an empty personal life, and blind ambition were all being discussed as possible reasons for Yelena's bizarre and vicious behavior. Annabelle could imagine the frenzy at the Broadcast Center, but she couldn't have cared less. Just as long as the police and FBI could build an airtight case against Yelena, a woman so driven and sick that murder seemed a reasonable solution to her.

Annabelle answered her cell phone, expecting her husband's call. Tara, fretting about her brother, had awakened crying from a bad dream last night, and Annabelle and Mike had agreed that it would be best if he stayed with their daughter at home while Annabelle went to the hospital to be with Thomas.

"Mike?"

"No, Annabelle. It's Wayne Nazareth. I just wanted to see how your son is."

Annabelle was touched by the gesture of the young man, a twin himself. Wayne knew too well what tragedy was, how life could change in an instant, that a single event could send out ripples that affected the many lives that had to continue onward.

"Thomas is doing very well, Wayne. Thanks so much for calling."

"Can I do anything, Annabelle? Bring you anything?" he offered.

"That's so sweet of you, Wayne. But I think we're all set here."

"Okay, Annabelle. Take care of yourself... and your son."

"I will, Wayne. I will."

Santa Claus and his reindeer brought up the rear of the parade as the phone rang again.

"How's it going over there?" Mike asked.

"We're fine. Just fine." Annabelle's hand brushed the top of Thomas's head. "How are you and Tara?"

"We've been watching the parade, thinking of you. Mrs. Nuzzo called, and she's bringing over some turkey and stuffing later."

"This was one way to get out of cooking a Thanksgiving dinner," Annabelle joked feebly. "We have so much to be thankful for, don't we, Mike?" she whispered, feeling her throat constrict. Thomas was going to pull through, and Annabelle was sure that Mike too was going to be all right.

She listened as her husband answered with the old steady confidence in his voice. "Yes, baby. We do."